Family Survival:

A Family's Apocalypse

Apocalypse: A Family's Survival Story

by

A J Newman

This book is a work of fiction. All events, names, characters, and places are the product of the author's imagination or are used as fictitious events. That means that I thought up this whole book from my imagination, and nothing in it is true.

To contact the Author, please leave comments @

https://www.facebook.com/aj.newmanauthor.5?ref=bookmarks

*

Acknowledgments

This book is dedicated to Patsy, my beautiful wife of thirty-six years. She assists with everything from Beta reading to censor duties. She enables me to write, golf, and enjoy my life with her and our mob of Shih Tzu's.

Thanks to Dee at <u>Dauntless Cover Design</u> for the fantastic cover.

AJ Newman

Table of Contents

Books by AJ Newman. 3 1

Prologue. 5..3

Chapter 1. 8 5

Chapter 2. 24 20

Chapter 3. 36 31

Chapter 4. 44 39

Chapter 5. 59...53

Chapter 6. 65 58

Chapter 7. 87...80

Chapter 8. 114..107

Chapter 9. 123..116

Chapter 10. 133..126

Chapter 11. 147..139

Chapter 12. 167..159

Chapter 13. 180..172

Chapter 14. 199..190

Chapter 15. 208..199

Chapter 16. 233..223

Chapter 17. 251..240

Books by AJ Newman. 260 249

About the Author. 262 251

*

Books by AJ Newman

Old Man's Apocalypse:
Old Man's War
Old Man's Journey

Prepper's Apocalypse
Prepper's Apocalypse
Prepper's Apocalypse: Collapse
Prepper's Apocalypse: Betrayal

John Logan Mysteries" The Human Syndrome

Extinction Level Event
Extinction
Immune: The Hunted

War Dogs
Heading Home
No One Left Behind
Amazon Warriors

EMP:
Perfect Storm
Chaos in the Storm

Cole's Saga series:
Cole's Saga
FEMA WARS

American Apocalypse:
American Survivor
Descent into Darkness
Reign of Darkness
Rising from the Apocalypse

After the Solar Flare:
Alone in the Apocalypse
Adventures in the Apocalypse

Alien Apocalypse:
The Virus
Surviving

A Family's Apocalypse Series:
Cities on Fire
Family Survival

The Day America Died:

New Beginnings
Old Enemies
Frozen Apocalypse

The Adventures of Jon Harris:
Surviving
Hell in the Homeland
Tyranny in the Homeland
Revenge in the Homeland
Apocalypse in the Homeland
John Returns

AJ Newman and Mack Norman
Rogue's Apocalypse:
Rogues Origin
Rogues Rising
Rogues Journey

A Samantha Jones Murder Mystery:
Where the Girls Are Buried
Who Killed the Girls?

These books are available on Amazon: https://www.amazon.com/AJ-Newman/e/B00HT84V6U/ref=dp_byline_cont_ebooks_1

To contact the Author, please leave comments @
https://www.facebook.com/aj.newmanauthor.5?ref=bookmarks

*

Prologue

Most of my novels have a strong central character who is the hero of the story. This book tells the story of a family who has to deal with a world that has fallen apart and survived in its ashes. The Karr family is the "hero" in this tale, and together they can overcome all odds to help each other live through the horrible events that occur during an apocalypse.

Family doesn't always mean blood kin. The Karr family grows as time goes on and with each new member, it grows stronger.

This is a series about how the Karr family survives and meets the challenges thrown at them during the early days of the Apocalypse. There have been nuclear and EMP attacks on the USA and most of the world. The Apocalypse has caught the world by surprise. Cities and countries are on fire. The USA has been reduced to burned-out cities, the grid is down, and society has reverted backward 150 years. Food and drinkable water are scarce. The US Government is no longer able to help or protect its citizens. Millions are dying.

In **"Cities on Fire,"** the Karr family survived the first week of the apocalypse and all arrived at the family bugout location. During that week, they experience the best and the worst of what mankind has to offer when the shit hits the fan.

In **"Family Survival,"** several members of the Karr family have been arrested as looters and sent to a FEMA camp. The rest of the Karr family fights off the hordes of starving people who are flooding out of the large cities. One of the Family members travels to the FEMA camp to rescue her Mom and son and has to fight her way there and back. To make things worse a crooked Senator and Sheriff want to take the family's crops, weapons, and land.

What would you do to survive?

The Karr family has a mixture of old-school preppers, conservatives, and liberals, making for an exciting blend of personalities, opinions, and sometimes even volatility. They can hate the sin but always love the sinner who disagrees. They have each other's backs through thick and thin.

AJ Newman

Character List

Josephine Karr is a Policewoman, Bill's wife and mother to Will, Missy, and Jake.

Bill Karr – He is a Nurse and Josephine's husband. He is the liberal in the family.

Will Karr – He is the oldest at 16. He has been trained in prepping by his Papaw Bob.

Missy Karr – She is 15 and a tomboy.

Jake Karr – He is 12 and a couch potato.

Bob Karr – Bill's father and is a widower. He is a retired Army Officer and very conservative.

Jane Carter – Josephine's mother. She is a nurse and works with Bill at the local hospital.

Maddie O'Berg – The Senator's daughter. The girl who helps Jane and the Kids and joins the Karr Family.

Walt Long – Jo's partner who loves her and wants her to leave Bill and marry him. They got too close, and Jo backed away. He is an ex-Army MP.

Barry O'Berg – US Senator from Tennessee. Crooked politician and power hungry man who wants to build his empire from the ashes.

Jim Dickerson – A farmer east of Lebanon who becomes a leader in the resistance against the Senator.

Jack Fulkerson – Ex-Army man who lives in the area and joins Bob's team.

Joan Gregory – One of Maddie's teachers who becomes one of the Karr family.

*

Chapter 1

Day 8 – And We're Here to Help You!

Jane woke up before the others, looked at Bob lying in her arms, and wondered what he would think if he knew she was the person dressed in black killing the assholes around the Horseshoe. She looked over to Will and Maddie's bunk and made eye contact with Maddie. She was awake, and Will was snuggled up against her back with his arms around her. Maddie smiled and waved at Jane.

"Good morning Mamma Jane."

"Good morning, children," she said with a laugh and then added, "I guess we'll find out what they have in store than us."

"Anything beats breaking rocks out in the hot sun as you see in the old westerns," replied Maddie.

Will was also awake with his arm around Maddie, with Maddie's head was on his other arm. He hugged her and wondered what was going through her mind as he prayed that she would love him as much as he loved her. He said an extra prayer that they would all return safely and that everyone in the Horseshoe was safe.

The past week was a blur in Will's mind as he sorted through the events. They had walked hundreds of miles to safety, killed several men, saved the lives of several of his family, and met the woman of his dreams. The good outweighed the bad.

They lay peacefully in their slumber for a few minutes before they were blasted out of their bunks at 5:00 sharp by bugles and then the announcer told them to shit, shower and shave by 5:30 when breakfast would be served.

After breakfast, they found out what recreation the Army had in store. They were forced to line up outside by a group of parked semi-trailers and handed shovels, rakes and hoes as they passed by the end of the trailers. They were then led out to a vast garden covering 50 acres, and they were given assignments. The men were tasked to dig a shallow drainage ditch around the whole garden while the women were told to hoe the weeds between the neat rows of the garden. The work started at 6:30, and the guards gave some direction; however, a few trusted prisoners led the effort. They reminded everyone that they were growing the food they needed to survive this winter.

Bob had given instructions to cozy up to their fellow workers and get as much information as possible about the camp and the surrounding area. A young lady started talking to Will, and he pumped her for information. She had been through Cherokee many times before the lights went out and were from Kentucky. Will was talking with her while he assembled a map of the area in his mind.

"Will, do you have a girl?"

"No," he said, then caught himself and replied, "Well yes, but it's a weird story."

"So maybe you have a girl, or maybe you don't have a girl."

Maddie had been working toward Will and the girl since she spotted him talking to her. She overheard the conversation and walked between the two of them and said, "Will has a girl, and it's me. Will, I'm so sorry about being mean to you. You are mine, and I'll be better to you."

Maddie led him away from the girl holding Will's hand. Will pulled her to a stop away from the young woman and said, "Maddie, what was that about. I still care about you, but I know I must move on. She was a sweet girl...."

"Will, I know that I've been driving you crazy, but seeing you with her made me very jealous, and I finally realized how much I care for you. I want to be your girlfriend and see where we go from there. Please don't be mad at me. After all, we've only known each other for a short time."

Will replied, "Maddie, I have only known you for a few days but fell in love with you right after we met. Don't say anything you don't mean." Will said as he snuck a kiss and then walked off to get back to work.

They worked without a break until 11:30, when they were marched past a series of water-filled tubs with soap and towels beside them. There was a bit of shuffling of people as the men and women tried to find their mates.

Bob found Jane first, and they helped Will find Maddie and then got back in line for chow. The meal was a scoop of beans, two hot dogs, a slice of bread, and water. They were famished and didn't talk much as they stuffed the food in their mouths. They finished early and went outside to mill around with the others as they waited to return to their jobs.

Will saw a young guard and said, "Aren't you from Lexington?"

"Yes, do I know you?"

"Yes, you pitched against Louisville Male during the regionals. I hit a home run in the eight, but y'all beat us 5-1."

"Yes, I remember that. You spoiled my no-hitter."

"When did you join the Army?"

"Earlier this year, I tore my arm up, dropped out of college, and joined the Army. Why are you here?"

"My family was searching for some clothing, and the Blackman Troops thought we were looters."

"They say everyone is a looter. The truth is that FEMA needs people to grow these crops, or the nation will starve."

"That doesn't make sense. We are farmers and were growing crops on over 150 acres. Those idiots are hurting the farming effort. We were growing a hundred times the food we needed to survive. We planned to trade food for gas, oil, and labor once the crops came in. There were less than 30 people actually farming, and there are thousands here. How many of these gardens are there?"

"There are ten of them planned for here, and there are only ten FEMA camps like this one around the country. Most of them were burned to the ground by the swarms of people who left the cities to find food. Blackman Troops killed hundreds of thousands of them, but there were just too many, and they overwhelmed FEMA and the Military. The government is holed up under a mountain, and the cities have burned to the ground. There are millions of people still on the road. The Major is afraid they will overrun this camp."

"Wow, what does he plan to do?"

"There will be too many to fight. We'll probably retreat to a safer place and start over. The river protects us from the north, and we're off the beaten path, so perhaps we'll survive here."

The Sergeant of the Guards was making his rounds, so they cut the conversation short. Will gave the others the highlights and said, "We need to escape before this camp is overrun by walkers from the north."

Bob replied, "I have a plan, and if it works, we'll be on the road in two to three days. Now here are my plans.

***

There were no volunteers, so Jo packed her Bugout Bag, extra ammunition, and food for her trip; she only took one bag of dog food since Max would find his food on the way. Cherokee was only 160 miles from Dixon Springs, and she was taking Bob's old pickup with an extra 20 gallons of gas. She also brought several boxes of trade goods to help buy anything else she needed along the way.

She planned to drive straight through, hide the truck close to the camp and figure out how to free her family from FEMA. She told her husband to watch over Jake and Missy and left at sundown.

***

It was the end of the day, and the prisoners were walking back to their tents when Will saw Maddie up ahead. She was talking with a guard and was looking very mad.

"Keep your hands to your damn self," Maddie said to the guard.

The guard grabbed her butt and said, "You'll do what I say when I say."

Will flew through the air, tackled the guard, knocked him down, and said, "If you touch my wife again, I'll kill you.

The guard raised his rifle, but Will was faster and grabbed the barrel, yanked it from the man's hands and threw it across the courtyard. The guard pulled his pistol and tried to point it at Will when Will's right foot whipped out and kicked it from his hands.

Will was hit on the head from behind by two more guards, and he fell to the floor.

The Sergeant of the guards yelled, "Don't hurt him."

A young lady yelled, "He was only defending his wife. The guard assaulted her, and I'm going to tell my Dad."

She was the young lady flirting with Will earlier that morning. By now, Maddie was in tears and had fallen to the ground beside Will. She had Will's head on her lap and inspected the gash on the back of his head. He was awake but groggy. Maddie looked up at the woman and thanked her for speaking up.

The guards pulled her away and took Will to the medics but allowed Maddie to follow them to the waiting room. Will was lightheaded, but the doctor told Maddie that he should be okay in a day or two.

Sergeant Hines, "What happened, and why did that young man attack an armed guard?"

"Major, Private Wells was making advances toward the boy's wife, and the boy jumped Wells."

"You are telling me that a young unarmed man took away the Privates weapons and beat the hell out of him single-handedly."

"Sir, I was there. The Private grabbed the girl's ass. Her husband leaped through the air and tackled the Private. The Private tried to shoot the boy with his rifle. The boy took the rifle from him and threw it across the courtyard, and the Private then drew his pistol. The boy turned and kicked the gun away. That's when Privates Malloy and Martin knocked the boy down with a butt stroke to the head."

"That's exactly what my daughter saw. What do we do?"

"Court-martial Wells and give a medal to the boy. His name is Will Karr."

"I agree on the court-martial, but we can't give the boy a medal even if he did us a favor. That asshole was a ticking time bomb. Do whatever it takes to get rid of him. Send him on a one-man mission to California to ask for more troops."

"Will do."

"Make sure the boy is getting the best medical aid we have to offer. My daughter has taken an interest in the couple. Oh, if you see her out mingling with the prisoners, please send her butt back to my tent."

"Yes, sir."

"Now another topic; have there been any significant findings from your scouting squads or our internal spy network?"

"Sir, nothing promising from the scouts, but there are two different prisoners in the camp that were taken away from thriving communities. Jake Simpson and Bob Karr are both the doomsday prepper types. Simpson led a band down from Indianapolis and started farming in mid-Alabama, close to Birmingham. Bob Karr lives in a small farming community and has fields planted and developed a good security force."

"How did you get the detail?

"We identified several targets and bugged their bunks. The young man who beat up Wells is Karr's son or grandson. He knew one of our guards before the shit hit the fan and opened up to him. That's why I was close by when Wells got out of line."

"What a small world."

"How many men and women do we have in our band?"

"Four men, counting us and three women counting your daughter. There are two children."

"Have everyone ready to march in two days. We'll roll out by 2300. Have a Humvee and a deuce and a half stocked with food, weapons, and ammo. It's time to put our operation into phase one. Tell Lieutenant Smith to come to my office."

Lieutenant Smith arrived at the Major's office a few minutes later, and the Major asked Smith to join him in a glass of whiskey. Smith asked, "Sir, what's the occasion?"

"Dick, you are being promoted to Captain and will take command of the camp tomorrow. It would please me if you wore my Captain's bars that I received upon my promotion to Captain."

"Sir, this is a surprise."

"Yes, son, it is. I have been called back to headquarters for a new mission, taking several high-value detainees with me. Headquarters has been looking for these people all week, and they arrived a day ago. It's hush-hush, or I'd explain in more detail."

"Thanks for the confidence. I won't let you down."

"I know you won't. Dismissed."

"Sir, how did it go with the Lieutenant?"

"I gave him a promotion to Captain and placed him in charge of the camp."

Hines laughed and said, "I'll bet he almost peed himself like a puppy when you put the bars on his collar."

"Yep, the brown-nosing bastard thinks he's the big man on campus. Too bad the campus is closing its doors in a couple of days."

***

"Mrs. Karr, keep talking to him to keep him awake. We will check on him frequently to ensure that he doesn't have a concussion. The blow only glanced off his head with the full impact on his left shoulder. Sorry, we don't have any of the x-ray, CT scan or other equipment working, so it's back to the turn of the century medical practice for the foreseeable future."

Maddie thanked the doctor and looked down at Will as he left to perform his daily rounds. She looked into his eyes and felt such a fool to have told him that he was not her type. She wanted him to be her boyfriend, but he used the love word, which scared her. Thanks to her piece of crap father, she didn't trust any man.

"Maddie, what happened after I kicked the gun out of the soldier's hand?"

"Two soldiers came up from behind, and one of them hit you with his rifle, and then the medics brought you here."

"I guess I'm in big trouble with the Army."

"Maybe, but you are a hero to me. That asshole grabbed my ass and tried to fondle me. I tried to fight him off, and then you flew through the air and tackled him."

"I couldn't stand him putting his hands on you."

"So I'm your official girlfriend now."

"That's what you said when you got jealous when I was talking to that cute girl."

"She was homely at best and not up to your high standards."

"You are right. Now we both have been hit in the head with a gun. I wonder who has the hardest head."

"No question about it; you do."

They were interrupted when Sergeant Hines walked up and introduced himself, "Mr. and Mrs. Karr, I'm Sergeant Hines, and I'm here to apologize for the inexcusable behavior of Private Wells. He has been disciplined for the attack on Mrs. Karr."

"Thanks, I'm surprised at the apology but very thankful," said Will, then he added, "What's going to happen to us. We have a great community farming over a hundred acres and working with the surrounding people to expand that by tenfold. We don't need to be taking your food or time."

"I like that. You got straight to the point. Now I have to do the same. What do we do to a young man that attacked one of my soldiers?"

"I don't know what you will do, but you should give Will a medal. What would you do if the same soldier had his hands all over your wife's ass," asked Maddie?

"Lady, that was the mitigating factor. Any man worth his salt would have beat the soldier senseless. I have recommended that we give Will a slap on the wrist in front of the detainees and a handshake for helping us get rid of a Congressman's worthless piece of shit son who was good at getting away with violations such as you encountered. No one would stand up for themselves."

Will added, "The only thing we are guilty of is taking some clothes from a shop that had been looted and vandalized. I don't know if the Army got the message, but the world went to shit several days ago and won't ever be the same again."

The Sergeant thought for a minute then asked, "Would you ask your uncle if the both of you could meet with me and the Major to discuss a mutually beneficial solution to both our troubles?"

"I will be glad to ask as soon as I get out of here."

"I'll tell the doctor to release you now and have a medic check on you at your bunk a few times."

"Thanks."

"I'll check back with you after breakfast tomorrow."

***

"Hi, Papaw and Grandma. We're back," Will said as Maddie helped him walk to their bunk.

Bob and Jane were surprised to see Will and Maddie back that night. Jane rushed over and helped Maddie get Will into the bed and under the covers.

Will said, "Y'all do know that I'm okay and just got a bump on my head. My shoulder took the full blow. My shoulder hurts, but the pain meds have that dulled down."

Bob shook his hand and said, "I'm surprised they don't have you chained to a hospital bed since you beat up that guard."

Maddie said, "Bob, Sergeant Hines gave us an apology from the Major who runs this camp for his man assaulting me. They will only tell the camp that Will was protecting me and should have used better judgment before attacking the soldier."

Will waved for his Grandma and Papaw to come closer so they wouldn't be overheard and then said, "The Major wants to meet with Papaw and me tomorrow to discuss a mutually beneficial solution to both of our troubles. He mentioned you by name Papaw."

"Did he mention what the troubles were?"

"No, he was kinda' mysterious. I told him I would discuss it with you and give him an answer in the morning," Will replied.

Jane asked, "Do they know that none of us are actually married?"

"I don't think so, but does that matter. You and Papaw are getting married soon, and Maddie and I are committed to each other. What concerns me is that they know a lot more about us than we do about them," Will said as he placed his finger over his lips and motioned for a pencil and paper.

He wrote, **"Could this placed be bugged?"**

Bob answered with, **"Yes! Look for bugs after lights out."**

Bob changed the subject and said, "We definitely want to meet with the Major and see what he thinks. Now it's just about lights out, and Will needs his rest."

Jane added, "Maddie tell me about being committed to each other in the morning," as she hugged her Grandson goodnight.

All four searched their bunk area for bugs for several minutes when Maddie poked Will and whispered, "There is an odd object on the bed frame above our heads."

Will threw a sock and hit Bob. Bob looked over, and Will pointed to the bed frame above and pointed at his lips and ears. Bob gave the okay sign.

Will felt Maddie moving and wiggling in the bed behind him and rolled over to see what was wrong. Maddie pressed her naked body against him and whispered in his ear.

"Will I love you, and I'm sorry for being such a bitch. I'll take good care of you from now on. Kiss me."

*

Chapter 2

Day 8 – The Walkers

By the eighth day, more and more people had run out of food or were driven from their homes by starving people trying to steal their food. Of course, there were small pockets of preppers across the country that had prepared for this very situation and had plenty of food, water, and guns. For the most part, they were keeping their heads down and letting the "Big Die Off" run its course.

A third of the country didn't have a week's food supply in their houses. They were the ones who joined in the looting of Kroger's, Walmart's, and other grocery stores. The fifth-generation government assistance people who relied on food magically supplied by their EBT cards caused the worst issues. Many had never worked a day in their lives, and others had been employed at jobs that didn't prepare them for survival.

The icing on this crap cake was that the hoods, thugs, biker gangs, and criminals had guns and were organized. They took what they wanted in the cities and took charge of most large food, water, medical supplies, drugs, and alcohol supplies.

The stores were looted first, then warehouses and private homes before the masses from the city began leaving to find food in the countryside. Many city people thought that every farm had cows, pigs, and chickens and a cornucopia of fresh vegetables just for the picking. The progressive liberals who fought so hard for gun control had no guns; the scumbags who they wouldn't keep in jail quickly killed them off. Many died because of that wrongheaded thinking. Karma is a bitch!

***

"John, I ran into a roadblock above Lebanon where one of the guards told me about a farming community below Dixon Springs that had food, water, women, and electricity."

"And Tiny, exactly why did this want to be cop tell you this story," asked the leader of the drug gang."

"John, I traded that redhead to him for some 9mm ammo, and he did me a solid," replied Tiny, who then added, "It's on our way. Let's check it out."

"On that, I agree. We've added twenty fighters and seven chicks to the family. We got to feed them somehow. I want to start my own kingdom down here in the south. That place could be it. Send ten of our best to scout out the place."

***

"Jack, the number of Walkers, has begun to dramatically increase, and many are dirty, hungry, and mad as hell at the world. I talked with a few from as far north as Cincinnati. They all tell the same story of looting, riots, and violence. They all hope to find a farm with plenty of food. The funny thing is that we also have about a quarter of the people heading north to find food."

"Yeah, the whole damn country is in the same boat."

"So far, we've been able to scare most away with a few shots over their heads, but these people are getting more aggressive and demanding entrance to our community. I don't know if the guards can actually shoot these poor people."

"The first thing is to stop thinking of them as poor people. They will kill you for your food. I'll go to the gate and give the guards a pep talk and increase the number of guards until the flow subsides. It's just a matter of time until they try to overpower us and dozens get killed," Jack responded.

Greg replied, "I just don't know if our team can shoot hundreds of starving people. Several have mentioned sharing our food."

"That would be a disaster. They will do what it takes to keep their kids and loved ones from starving. Feel sorry for the Walkers but don't give them food. That would cause the herd to crash through the gates. Who wants to share our food?"

"The Nelsons and the Grinnells."

"They would have been my first guess. We have to keep their bleeding heart crap from infecting the rest of the team."

"Several others are listening to them."

"Damn."

***

A messenger showed up on Jim's doorstep the night before with a note from his old friend Ben.

The message said, 'I received your letter concerning the people in the Horseshoe. I agree that we need to hook up with them and form an alliance. Meet with them and develop a relationship. Can you hold Lebanon off until we arrive? Send your reply with the messenger. She can be trusted. Ben.'

Jim wrote his reply and decided that he needed to visit Bob and the people in the horseshoe and see what Karr's people have done since the shit hit the fan.

***

Jack drove north to the gate and saw hundreds of people yelling and screaming at the guards.

"How do these people know to turn south at Dixon Springs and come here?"

"There are signs east of Dixon Springs that tell them to come here. One man told me the Hartsville Police said there was food here."

Several guards came over to Jack, and the leader said, "Jack, we need to give them some food, so they'll move on."

"That would be a disaster. A couple of hundred piled up along the fence, and if you tried to give out food, they would overwhelm you and take over the Horseshoe. Millions of people are on the roads looking for food, and we can't feed them all. Any food you give them is food that could have fed our families. One day we will have extra, and we will trade it to our neighbors for things we need."

"What if we decide to give some of our own food to these poor people?"

"That would be very kind of you and also idiotic. We only have enough food to make it until the crops come in. Besides, you would be overrun and trampled to death."

"Hey, Jack! Look!"

Jack turned and saw several men had a telephone pole, and they were heading toward the gate to ram it down.

Jack yelled for his men to run to the gate as he shot three times into the air.

"Put that pole down and get the hell out of here. All of you. We don't have any extra food, and you have been tricked."

One man responded, "You can't shoot all of us. Ram the gate."

"I'll shoot you first, and then any man or woman who tries to go through the gate."

The mouthy man yelled, "Ram the gate," and a dozen men ran with the pole aimed at the gate. Jack leveled his AR, aimed, and pulled the trigger three times. The leader and his most vocal supporters dropped dead. Jack killed the last armed man then yelled at the people on the ground cowering in fear, "Get out of here, or we will shoot you.

Jack fired several bullets into the ground, and the people fled. One man waved his fist and yelled, "We'll be back."

Jack shot him in the face and yelled, "If you want to die, come on back. We will kill anyone who approaches our fence from now on. Get going."

The area was quickly deserted, and Jack went to see how the wounded guard was doing. The lady had a wound to her right arm and was bedridden for a week while she mended.

George Nelson and Gig Grinnell walked up to Jack, and George said, "That was murder. You had no right shooting those men. They just want to feed their families."

Jack replied, "You two were invited to join the community and can be sent packing if you keep this shit up. We are not going to share our food with those outsiders. If you keep this crap up, I personally will run your asses out of the Horseshoe and send you back to your homes in Dixon Springs."

"You can't do that."

"I can, and I will. Get out of my sight before something bad happens to you whiny, assed people."

The two ran away and complained to everyone they saw on their way home. Greg had joined in shooting the attackers but wasn't happy with how Jack handled the two.

"Jack, don't you think we should use a bit of diplomacy handling the people of our community?

"No, I don't. Those people need to be run off before they get us killed or give our food away."

"Jack, I know they are wrong, but why make enemies out of them?"

"They are enemies of the community, and we should never have let them live here. Everyone knew they were bleeding heart liberals and would cause problems. Why let rattlesnakes loose in the chicken coop?"

George Nelson and Gig Grinnell went door to door, telling everyone that Jack executed several innocent people who just asked for food to feed their starving children. They also planted the seeds that Bob and Jack should be removed from power. Most people knew these troublemakers and ignored them and their false statements; however, a fourth of the community was very concerned that their security people were gunning down poor innocent people.

A large handful of people complained to Greg and asked for a community meeting to see what had actually happened and what Greg would do about the alleged massacre. Greg told them that they had only heard half-truths and would schedule a town meeting in two days to discuss the issues.

***

Jack went back home and vented on his son Tony and their wives. They agreed with him, and Tony said, "Dad, we may have to leave this group if those idiots get their way. The first attempt at a food giveaway will be a total disaster. Thousands of people will hear about it and flood the place. We could all be killed. Dad, don't back down from this fight. If Bob were here, he'd slap some sense into these bastards."

"I know we are right, but Greg is too nice, and I'm afraid he'll listen to those do-gooders and do something stupid before Bob gets back," Jack replied.

"Dad, what can we do? The Walkers are getting bolder, and I've seen signs that someone may be directing them to come to us for food."

"I agree. It probably is the same people over in Hartsville. We may have to go over there and clean their clocks when Bob gets back. I think we need to split up and have one of us on the wall all of the time."

"I think that's a good idea. I'll take the night shift since old people need their rest."

"Thanks, son."

Jack had only been asleep for a short time when Tony called him on the walkie-talkie, "Dad, you'd better get over here quick. I'm on the east bank about halfway to the wall. The bastards drug twenty or thirty boats down to the water and are coming across to attack below the wall. We're lucky our horseback patrol saw them."

"Greg, Izzy, get your teams and meet me there. We need to shoot them before they get ashore."

Jack arrived, and Tony gave him the binoculars to scan the shore. Jack saw a few men and women milling around and wondered where the invasion force was. There were barely enough people to fill one boat, much less twenty.

Jack had a terrible thought, "This is a diversion. They are going to hit us somewhere else. Guards, do you see anything suspicious along the wall?"

"Tower 1, nothing to see here."

"Tower 2, we haven't seen anything.

"Tower 3, same here we... wait, there's some movement in the bushes across no man's land."

"What do you see?"

There were several loud metallic noises, and the guard at Tower 3 yelled, "Damn, they're shooting at me. Come quickly. They are running across the field."

"Shoot to kill the ones in front. All towers kill anyone in the no man's land. We're on our way."

Jack and Tony brought six men with them, and Greg had seven men and women. As the attackers climbed over the wall using ladders, they drove up. A dozen were on the ground and running toward the homes south of the barrier. The people were coming over the wall faster than they could shoot them, so Tony pulled out his ace in the hole.

"Dad, grab the Molotov cocktails from the back of the truck and start pitching them across the wall. Fry the bastards."

Izzy joined in the effort as the rest of the team kept shooting the people already across the wall. The firebombs were more effective than Tony dared to hope, and soon around sixty of the attackers were on fire and the entire area on the north side of the wall for the entire length was on fire. The invaders were stopped in their tracks.

"What the heck just happened?"

"Dad, that was my firewall."

It took another hour to mop up the men who climbed over the wall before they could take a break.

"Son, I get the firebombs, but why did the ground on the other side of the wall catch on fire and burn so vigorously?"

"When I went back to the gate after I left you, I thought that it would be a bad time for someone to make another attack. I took a tractor with a 500-gallon tank of diesel fuel mixed with oil and gas and then sprayed as far as the crop sprayer would shoot the fuel. I sprayed the entire thousand yards along the fence."

"Damn, it worked, but I don't know if I'll ever get the smell of burning human flesh out of my nose again. Perhaps we could use the sprayers to make a flame thrower," Jack replied.

"Dad, I know I should feel bad, but the "Walking Democrats" are learning about Darwin's theory of natural selection first hand."

"Son, I hate that all these people are dying off, but most were living off the government tit and didn't have any practical skills. Remember, I'm a Democrat or was before the shit hit the fan, so keep that shit to yourself."

*

Chapter 3

Day 9 – Mama Bear

Jo remembered that the city of Hartsville would be challenging to go through, so she took the same route that Harold's team used to evade the barricades on their way home from scavenging. She avoided the barrier closest to the bridge by cutting through a field and a stand of trees by the river on the west side of the bridge. Before daylight, she drove very slow as she pulled onto the road. The two Deputies manning the barricade never heard her go away.

Jo knew she had to avoid all of the larger cities, so she worked her way southeast around Lebanon on the backroads. Her plan was to get around Lebanon to Highway 840, safely around Nashville, and then work her way south toward Florence, Alabama.

The entire drive to Florence would usually take about three hours, but by taking the back roads, avoiding people along the way, and dodging stalled cars, the trip would take as much as ten times as long. Jo was only nine miles below Hartsville when she began wondering if the journey was even possible. Even the back roads had people flooding into the countryside scrounging for food and water. Most got out of the way as she drove towards them; however, the more desperate ones tried to stop her, and several took potshots at her when she didn't stop.

One group tried to use its bodies as a human roadblock. Jo slowed and waved her AR at them, but they wouldn't move out of the road. One man who appeared to be their leader yelled, "Give us your truck, weapons, and food, and we will let you live."

Jo yelled back, "I only have enough food for myself, and I am searching for my son and father. Please let me head on south."

"Hell no. We are starving, and the damn government hasn't shown up to help us."

"Please don't make me shoot you. I'm a police officer and will shoot if you try to approach."

The man waved his pistol for the crowd to follow him to Jo. Jo took aim and shot him in the head. He fell a few feet from the others, and most ran. A woman ran to him, dropped to her knees, and placed his bloody head in her lap. She looked up and yelled at the remaining crowd to charge Jo. About eight began running at Jo with axes and a few guns. One man shot and hit the truck on the side. Jo jumped out, dropped to one knee, and started picking them off one by one until all eight were down. She reloaded her AR, got back in the truck, and headed through the bodies at full speed. The bumps and crunching noise almost made her sick. A couple of shots were fired at her, but they were wild and didn't get close to the vehicle. She drove on, passing a handful of people every mile or two. Most tried to flag her down, but she ignored them and kept moving.

She was three hours into her excursion and was only 15 miles from the bottom of the horseshoe. She headed due west below Lebanon to connect with Highway 840 and saw a crowd up ahead marching down Highway 40 towards her. She got off at the next exit, headed a short way south, and then worked east just below Highway 40 until she saw the junction for Highway 840. She put the old Ford into four-wheel drive and ran down the side of 840 until she saw a place without a guardrail and drove through the fence and up to the Highway.

Jo knew Bob would shit a brick when he saw the ruined paint on the truck; however, she had to do whatever it took to get her family back home safe. Then it hit her that was what most of the people she ran across were trying to do.

The trip's next leg took Max and her down Highway 840 between Smyrna and Murfreesboro. Thousands of workers were on their way to work at the dozens of warehouses, computer manufacturers, and other businesses when the lights went out. The road was a parking lot of cars, trucks, and semi-trucks, but she kept the truck moving and only had to fire a couple of warning shots to stop people from stopping her. The stalled vehicles tapered off when she got a few miles past the Highway 24 overpass and headed towards Highway 65 South. She picked up speed and was soon on Highway 65, heading toward the cut-off to Springfield, where she would catch Highway 43 South and head down to Florence.

Jo continued to dodge stalled vehicles and people wanting her truck or her food for the rest of the day. The going was slow, and she pulled off the road into the woods off Highway 43, about ten miles south of Lawrenceburg. Jo waited until there were no people in sight and pulled off the highway and down to a creek about a hundred yards off the road. She could see the bridge over the stream but was confident that no one passing by could see her or the truck from the road.

She placed her sleeping bag in the truck's bed and quickly fell asleep with Max at her side as the clouds moved out of the area and the stars were revealed. She woke to a strange sound, peered above the bed of the old Ford, and saw a light under the bridge. Jo tied her shoestrings, found her AR, and quietly slid off the truck's tailgate with Max leading the way.

She carefully walked through the woods to keep bushes between her and the campfire. She was about fifty yards away when she heard a child crying and other unidentifiable noises. She kept low to the ground and crawled within 50 feet of the fire when she heard.

"Shut that brat up, or I'll shut the little bitch up. I can't concentrate with the racket. Shut her up and come back in the tent."

Jo saw a person get out of a tent and walk to a smaller tent on the other side of the fire. The figure was dark until it stood by the smaller tent to open the flap. It was a naked woman standing in the light of the fire. Jo crawled closer and heard the woman trying to get several children to stop crying.

"Please stop crying. You know how mad he gets when you cry. Please stop for me."

The kids settled down, and the woman left them to go back to the man in the other tent. She ducked into the tent and said, "They will be quiet now."

"Good, get your ass on the mattress and make love to me."

"Do what you have to do, but this isn't loving. I'll do whatever you want. Just don't hurt my kids."

"I want you to love me."

"How can I love a man who killed my husband and rapes me every day?"

"Easy, if you don't, I'll shoot the boy. The girls will come in handy if I have to kill you."

Jo was now standing outside the tent and heard all of the conversation. She told Max to stay, lifted the tent flap, and saw the man on top of the young woman and her blood boiled. She placed her rifle against the tent, drew her hunting knife, and slowly stepped into the tent. The man was too busy to hear Jo sneak up behind him and straddle him. She brought the knife to his throat as she grabbed him by the hair and yanked his head backward.

Jo said, "You won't rape any more women, you son of a bitch. Go to hell bastard," as she pulled him off the woman by his hair. She kicked him and then asked, "Are you okay?"

The woman was crying as she shook from fear. She replied, "Please don't kill my children. I'll do whatever you want."

Jo turned her flashlight on and said, "I don't want to hurt you. I just didn't want that man ever hurting another woman. He's dead now."

"Are my kids okay?"

"Yes, they are where you left them. Do you have a place to go?"

"No. Our family was on vacation and driving back to Louisville from Mobile when the car stalled. We started walking home when this man attacked us. He killed my husband and forced the kids and me to go with him. I guess you heard enough to know what he wanted from me. I was just trying to keep him from hurting my kids."

"Don't worry. You did what any mother would do to protect her children. My name is Jo Karr, and I have to pull out in the morning. I'm trying to find my mother and my son. Do you have any food?"

"My name is Ann Fry, and my kids are Jeff, Brenda, and Bea. We don't have much food. Al would chain me to a tree and go out foraging every day but brought back less and less each day."

"If I give you some food, do you think you can stay hidden here until I come back in a few days? I'll take you and the children to my home on the other side of Nashville. We have plenty of food, and you will be safe there."

"Yes, I'd like that. How long will you be gone?"

"It should only take three to five days. If I'm not back on the fifth day, go find a place to live. I'll set several rabbit traps so you can stretch out the MREs I'm leaving with you. Can you skin and dress a rabbit?"

"I never have, but I will do anything to feed my kids."

Jo gave her a quick education on catching and skinning rabbits along with short survival training. Jo also taught her how to handle the pistols. The man had two loaded handguns and a backpack full of survival gear, so the woman was better prepared than most these days.

At first light, Jo and Ann buried the body under the bridge with rocks and as much dirt as they could pile over the man. Jo showed the woman how to run the traps and found they had already caught two good-sized rabbits. The woman skinned and dressed the rabbits with clumsiness but got better at handling the second one. Max watched intently and then went to get his own rabbit.

"Ann, move the tents over to where my truck is parked and don't have a fire at night. A small fire will be okay during the day if you keep it under that tree over there. The leaves will disperse the smoke."

They hugged, and Jo drove back north about a mile before entering the highway to make sure no one came looking for Ann and the kids.

*

Chapter 4

Day 9 - Escape

Will woke up early the following day with his shoulder throbbing and a mild headache. He was spooned up against Maddie with his arm around her waist and her head on his other arm. Maddie was sleeping a deep and contented sleep of a person with no worries. Will kissed her neck and gazed at her beautiful face in the soft glow of the dim lights hanging from the ceiling in the tent.

Will reflected back on the previous week with a mixture of pain, joy, and sorrow. Meeting Maddie was the best thing that had ever happened to him, but the whole world was falling apart all around him.

He looked across the aisle and saw his Grandparents peacefully sleeping in their bunk, and that reminded him that his family's world was not falling apart thanks to those two and his parents. He thought about what they had done to keep the family and the Horseshoe community safe. No, their world wasn't falling apart. It was just being built from scratch, and it would be a better place to live a few years from now.

Will stroked Maddie's dark brown hair and kissed her neck several times until he woke her up. She rolled over, wrapped both arms around him, and gave him a long kiss.

She whispered, "Will, we have to stop meeting like this, or things might happen."

"I'm kinda hoping that things will happen again like last night. Maddie, I love you and want to live the rest of my life with you."

"Will, that was fantastic. I just realized how much I care for you when I thought I could lose you to that woman yesterday. Give me some time. I don't trust men thanks to my rotten father, and it's hard for me to get close to men."

"I'm not just any man. I'm your boyfriend, and you can trust me."

"I hope after last night we are more than girlfriend boyfriend," she teased Will.

"Maddie, I love you and want you to stay with me forever."

"I'm trying. My Dad screwed every woman he met and left my Mom for a bitch half his age. Oh, he sent money and presents, but I have only seen him twice in the past two years."

"Maddie, that wasn't me."

"I know. Hold me and kiss me."

That was when Will knew that the Senator was Maddie's father.

They fell back asleep only to be jolted from their bunks by the sound of the bugles on the loudspeakers.

Jane dressed, walked over to Will and Maddie, and asked, "How's my boy doing this morning? You two were ... well ... restless last night. I hope your bump on the head didn't keep you up."

"Considering my shoulder and head still hurt, I'm doing okay. I wonder how Mom and Dad are doing back at the Horseshoe."

Bob replied, "They are worried for our safety and trying to get a team to come looking for us. We need to get back home quickly, or we could have two groups held hostage or lost."

Jane added, "I'd search forever to find one of you. I just hope the team doesn't get captured by the DHS."

"Let's go get breakfast and wait on the Sergeant to contact us."

Sergeant Hines and two soldiers walked up to their area before they had a chance to head to the mess hall and said, "I need you four to come with me. Don't give us any trouble."

Bob looked at the others with a frown on his face but waved them to fall in behind him as they were escorted to the Major's dining area.

"Sir, Sergeant Hines and the four detainees are reporting as ordered."

Dismissed," the Sergeant said to the two men, who promptly left.

The Major saluted and said, "Please join Sergeant Hines and me for breakfast. Sergeant, is the area secure?"

"Yes, sir."

"I'm Major Ben Payne, and I've been called up from the Kentucky National Guard for this disaster. I don't know what you have heard, but the short story is that the entire world is in the same boat. The fact is that we don't know what happened; we do know that the grid, electronics, and most vehicles are dead. The militaries of a few countries have a few hardened vehicles that are still in operation, but they are few and far between.

The USA is disintegrating as we speak. Our government does not have the willpower or resources to help its people. The military has suffered mass desertions as men and women struggle to get back to their families. Criminals, gangs, and well-meaning groups are forming their own little countries to enable them to survive. I plan to do the same."

"Why are you telling us this? What do you want from us?"

"My family's homestead is located about halfway between Hartsville and Lafayette, Tennessee. Yep in your neighborhood. A childhood friend of mine is Jim Dickerson, who owns most of the land across from Hartsville on the south side of the river. Now everyone, please eat while we talk."

A light came on in Bob's mind, and he said, "I met Jim Dickerson the day the shit hit the fan. We saved a few people from a plane crash."

"Well, Jim has kept me informed on what is happening around my place, and he says that you and your group are some of the good guys. I want to firm up a relationship that will mutually benefit our three groups and result in a safe area to live in for our families. There are some sick people out there. We have an asshole Senator that has taken over Lebanon, and he will be a force to reckoned with."

Bob replied, "I'd like to hear more, but first, why do you want to leave this camp. It appears to have everything you need."

"Bob, if you don't join us, I will have the Sergeant drop you off near your home, so there is no downside to you or your family. After this discussion, I can't let you back in the general population here at the camp. The information could cause chaos."

Bob looked the Major in the eye and replied, "I'm good with that. I hope the beds are wider."

"I've received orders to pull my men out and travel to a secret location on the east coast where our government is in hiding. They want to start a new country with the remaining resources and screw the rest of the country. About half of the military won't go along with that. We plan to leave tonight and take you with us. We have a small group here that will relocate to my homestead, and we want you to join in our larger effort to make Middle Tennessee a safe place to live."

"I can't speak for all of our people, but I like what I have heard, and I'm in if what you say is what you really mean and aren't trying to become some kind of military dictator."

"I guess the proof is in the pudding. You get out of this place, and I hope you join us."

"Sounds good to me. Will, what do you think?"

"I'm in, and it looks like we have two new allies."

Bob asked, "What's next?"

Hines answered, "You four eat up, get rested, and be ready to leave tonight. We will supply everything needed for the trip. I can't give you your exact same weapons, but we will have M4s, Glock 17s and plenty of ammo for you when we let you off at the Horseshoe."

Bob looked over at the Major and said, "So that's why you bugged our bunks. You wanted to see if we can be trusted."

"Are you ex-military?"

"82nd."

"Good man! We can use a man like you. What was your rank?"

"Lt. Colonel."

The Major saluted Bob and told them that the Sergeant would give them updates as needed.

***

Hines escorted them to a room in the Major's private tent and told them to make themselves comfortable. There were two larger beds and one single bunk like the one they had been sleeping in. The room also contained a table with snacks and drinks, a pile of magazines, and a bookshelf full of books.

Jane looked around and said, "I'm going to get caught up on my sleep," and laid down on one of the larger beds.

Bob started perusing through one of the magazines and sat down on the bed with Jane. Maddie and Will lay down on the bunk bed, cuddled up, and tried to sleep in their usual position.

"Children, there are two beds. Maddie, you can have your own bed."

Maddie laid her head on Will's chest and gave Jane the finger as she said, "Mom, we've gotten close over the past few days, and I like it."

"Me too," Will said as he rubbed Maddie's back.

Bob chuckled and said, "I'll bet. What are you two going to do when we get back home and Will's Mom hears about the sleeping arrangements?"

Maddie replied, "I think Jo will understand. We love each other, and no one knows how much time we have left on this Earth. We plan to live life to its fullest."

Lunch and dinner were served per the regular camp schedule without seeing anyone except the orderlies who served the food. Then at 9:00 pm, the Sergeant appeared and gave them an update.

"We are leaving after the guards are changed at midnight. We will take two Humvees and an M35 truck. Our cover story is that we have six captives who have intelligence vital to national security and take them to Memphis to get them passed on to Headquarters. We have two men that will head on to their home in Indiana, plus you four. Of course, we'll get lost along the way and disappear.

The deuce and a half will be loaded with supplies along with you four and the other two. Your weapons will be in the back of the deuce and a half."

"We're bored here and ready to go."

"I'll come back at 2330 with two guards to escort you to the vehicles, and there shouldn't be any trouble from the camp. Be ready for any and everything from the civilian population. Those folks are starving and desperate."

"Papaw, about how long will it take to get back to the Horseshoe?"

"My guess is the better part of the night. It's only a four-hour drive in a large truck; however, you saw how bad the roads are, and I believe the Sergeant is correct about being attacked by starving mobs. Chill a while longer and be prepared to go."

Will and Maddie passed the time playing checkers while Bob slept with his head on Jane's lap. The two and a half hours dragged on forever, but finally, the Sergeant and two female guards appeared to take them to the trucks.

They walked past the Humvee with the Major and his daughter. The girl waved at Will and said, "Hi, Will."

Will walked on as Maddie whispered, "Bitch."

They climbed into the back of the truck with four armed guards, and the small convoy drove toward the front gate. The guards challenged the lead vehicle and let them pass when they found that the Major was in the convoy.

Only a few people were walking on the roads, and the convoy could move along at a reasonable rate of speed. They slowed on the outskirts of Tuscumbia, where there was a roadblock in the middle of the highway.

The Sergeant walked up to the back of the truck and said, "Bob, there is a bad bunch up ahead who won't let us go through unless we give them one of our vehicles and half of our supplies."

Bob replied, "How many are manning the roadblock?"

"We count nine out in the open and think there are a dozen more behind some stalled cars."

Bob replied, "Well, we can't let these outlaws stop us this early. Let us out here, and we'll come up on their right flank and pick off a bunch of them, and perhaps the others will skedaddle out of here."

"Tom and Alice go with them. Bob is in command. We'll wait until you surprise them and then pick off any survivors if they stay and fight. Here take these Night Vision Goggles."

Bob and the others snuck away from the truck staying in the shadows as they worked their way around the roadblock and came in on its right side. The barrier was made up of several cars pushed across the road and had a string of vehicles blocking any path around it.

"Look, several men and women are sitting around that fire fifty yards back of the roadblock. They don't appear to be very concerned about us attacking them," said Jane.

"That's because they have a Ma Deuce sticking out of the back of that RV to the left of the roadblock. See that pickup out in front. It is shot full of holes. We'll take out the machine gun, and the rest will be easy."

Will looked around and found two mason jars and a garden hose.

"Papaw, "I'm making two Molotov Cocktails, and we are going to have an RV roast."

"Son, be careful. They aren't paying much attention, but if you're caught out in the open, it could get dicey."

"Papaw, when the RV blows up, start shooting."

Will and Maddie filled the jars from the nearest car's gas tank, cut holes in the lids and stuffed strips of their shirts into the holes. Will started to go without Maddie, and she quickly got out ahead of him as they slinked their way around the stalled cars to the RV.

Maddie was several feet ahead of Will when suddenly a man jumped out from behind a car, grabbed Maddie, and held her at knifepoint.

"My, my, what a sweet piece of meat I've found. I don't believe I'm going to share you with the others."

Will saw the man and charged up behind him. He grabbed his knife and stabbed the man in the side. Will pushed the blade up into the man's kidney and held him as he died. The man was so surprised he didn't utter a word.

Maddie tore a piece of her shirt off and bound Will's left hand tightly. She made Will close his hand around the cloth to stop the bleeding. They picked up the jars and headed to the RV. Maddie waved at Will and showed him that the RV's windows had been knocked out. They lit the makeshift fuses and threw the jars into the open windows close to the machine gun.

One of the jars exploded in flames instantly, and the RV had a fireball on the machine gun end of the RV; a few seconds later, the entire RV exploded in a mushroom of fire and smoke. A few men tried to get out of the RV, but they were on fire. Maddie and Will started shooting at the men and women by the fire from behind a cargo van and scattered them like ants.

Bob and the Major's teams saw the explosion and began picking off any assholes who were unlucky enough to make themselves targets. The fight was over as quickly as it started when the survivors waved a white flag, threw their guns down, and fled the scene.

Hines directed his driver to push the vehicles out of the way while Bob's team collected the arms and ammunition that the criminals had left.

"Sir, there are 39 dead, and we have two wounded women."

"How bad are they?"

"Not life threatening, but the trouble is that they were hostages. What do we do with them?"

"Jane overheard the conversation and said, "I'm a nurse. Let me examine them."

"Sorry, but we have to get back on the road."

"Put them in the back of the truck and give us a flashlight. I will patch them up, and then you can decide what to do with them. They were hostages."

"Private, make room for them and load them up into the truck. Get the nurse a First Aid kit. Good luck."

They all loaded back into the vehicles and headed below Muscle Shoals to Highway 101, where they headed north and crossed the river.

"The two women were a mother and daughter who had been captured by the gang that afternoon. They had been wounded when the group they were traveling with tried to walk around the roadblock.

"Hello, I'm Helen Jackson, and this is my daughter Gabby. Thanks for helping with our wounds."

Maddie introduced everyone, and Jane jumped into treating their injuries, which weren't too severe. Helen had a sprained ankle and a gash to the back of her head. Her daughter had a flesh wound on her back from a ricochet she received during the fight at the roadblock. Both would recover quickly.

One of the soldiers gave each woman an MRE, and they ate as though they had never seen food before. They were both dirty and worn out from their travels.

"Maddie, hold the flashlight while I clean this gash. I can suture it if the damn truck doesn't buck too much."

"Helen, where are you two from?"

"We live in Oregon but were on a trip to Mobile when we were stranded at the Huntsville Airport. I don't know if we'll ever get home. My husband passed away several years ago, and I was looking at moving to the Gulf Coast for a change of pace. I write romance novels for a living and work from home."

Helen asked, "Where are you guys from?"

Our family is spread out from Middle Tennessee through Northern Kentucky, and we are currently living in the Nashville area when we're not out rescuing damsels in distress," replied Jane.

"Thanks for saving us from those scumbags. They didn't beat me as long as I did whatever the leader wanted. I just hope I don't get pregnant. I won't even try to guess what would have happened to my daughter if you hadn't come along."

"Where will you be heading now that you are back on the road. We are moving to the Nashville area."

"I wish I knew. Obviously, we can't make it to Oregon or Mobile, for that matter. Right now, we'd settle for a place with food and a place to sleep."

"Would you be willing to work on a farm tending crops working from sun up to sundown," Bob asked?

"Yes! Neither of us is afraid of work. Gabby and I have a large garden in Medford, and Gabby works at a nursery tending the plants. I won't lie. We'd do about anything to get a safe place with food."

*

Chapter 5

Day 10 – They return.

Jack said, "Son, I'm going up to the gate to check on the guards; would you come with me."

They were only halfway there when there was a frantic call from Izzy at the gate. He said, "Send help. They're staging vehicles to hide behind as they snipe at our guards."

"We'll be there in five minutes, and I'll call out the rest of the guards. All guards come to the fence now. You heard Izzy. We are under attack."

Jack arrived and saw a wave of men charging the gates as men and women behind the cars sniped at the people from the Horseshoe. The cars were being pushed toward the gate, and five to six people were pushing while several others shot from behind the protection of the slow-moving vehicles.

Suddenly, a wave of people rushed toward the gate with their hands in the air. The guards wouldn't shoot the unarmed people, and Jack saw they would be overwhelmed in seconds. Jack began shooting the people closest to the gate. Tony and Izzy joined in. Soon, two dozen dead people piled up in front of the entrance, and there was a mad rush of most of the people away from the gate.

Suddenly three shots rang out and one of the guards dropped.

Jack yelled," Kill the SOBs.

Jack saw that several cars were now only 50 yards from the gate and killed one of the snipers with his first shot. Only three of the six guards fired at the attackers. The gunfire from behind the cars kept Jack and his men pinned down as two more cars were pushed toward the gate. Jack saw a dump truck backing across the open field toward him to make matters worse. The truck bed was filled with armed men, and they were using the thick steel bed to protect them from the guard's gunfire.

Several guards were down, and Jack picked up his radio and screamed, "All fighters to the gate. We're being overwhelmed. Get your asses here now."

Jack ran over to the guards that weren't shooting and yelled, "These assholes are going to kill you, and then your families. Either start shooting or join them. You either fight or die."

The three men reluctantly began firing at the enemy, but the team was losing the battle. A dozen men and women joined the fight, and the best they could do was hold the attackers at bay. The 9mm rounds just bounced off the dump truck bed, and the civilian .223s weren't much better. The cars had stopped advancing due to the guards shooting the tires and the men that pushed the cars; however, the dump truck was still slowly moving closer.

It had been stopped a couple of times when the guards in the tower killed several of the drivers. More men just took their place, and the truck continued the attack. The dump truck was only a few yards from the gate as the battle became touch and go as to who would win when the truck suffered several explosions. The entire battlefield in front of Jack was riddled with heavy machine gun fire. All of the men behind the cars and the people in the dump truck were dead.

Jack saw a Humvee with a turret mounted machine gun firing at the men massed toward town, getting ready to charge the fence. The men and women fell like trees in a southern tornado. Another Humvee joined in and chased the people out of sight. The rat, a tat tat of the machine gun, continued for several minutes from the direction of Dixon Springs.

The first Humvee rolled to a stop by the gate and Bob, and a soldier jumped out and walked to the gate.

Bob said, "Looks like y'all been a bit busy lately. I'm sorry we ended your little turkey shoot, but I had to get my family back home and didn't want to wait for you to kill all of this riff raft."

"Thank God y'all arrived. They were overpowering us and would have overrun us in a few minutes."

"Greg, where are the rest of the fighters? Didn't you call all hands on deck?"

"About a third didn't get here."

"How long ago did you put the first call out? We heard several of your pleas for help twenty minutes ago. Everyone should have been here in ten minutes."

Greg stuttered and finally said, "I think a couple of our men talked some of our team from fighting. They told everyone that we were killing innocent people."

"Jack, why didn't you shoot the SOBs?"

"Jack wanted to, but I wouldn't let him. I thought we could reason with them," Greg replied.

"Well, damn it, Greg. You almost got everyone killed."

"I'm sorry. I was wrong. I think most of us never saw the threat as clearly as you and Jack did. I would have never believed those people would run into gunfire just to get our food."

"You've never starved before or watched your kids slowly die. Greg, this can never happen again, or people die."

Bob was interrupted as the deuce and a half truck drove up, and Jane, Maddie, and Will climbed down and joined the group.

"Oh my God. What happened?"

"The team fought off some very desperate people, and we helped finish off the resistance. Let's go home and get a bath and a change of clothes. Jack, please bring anyone twelve or above up here in the next hour to see what happens when you let your heart overrule your head. How many wounded and dead on our side?"

"One dead and six wounded."

"Are you and Izzy in the count?"

"Well, no, we only got hit by ricochets."

"Don't downplay your wounds. People will be dying from less after we run out of antibiotics."

"Tell everyone that I will conduct a meeting at 8:00 am sharp and don't be late. Make sure those do-gooder clowns are present and upfront. Oh, I'm very sorry. I forgot to introduce Major Ben Payne. We met him at a FEMA camp, and he and his group are joining us for a short while and then heading on to their home."

Jack, Greg, this is Helen Jackson and her daughter Gabby. They will join us and will stay in a trailer at my place until we sort things out. Greg, please have the team move two more extra campers over to my place.

*

Chapter 6

Day 10 – Bob Takes Charge

Jo headed south on Highway 43 and continued to encounter desperate people and stalled cars along her journey. She got off Highway 43 and headed over to Highway 101, hoping to have an easier time crossing the 101 bridge instead of the bridge in Florence, which was in the middle of several cities. The bridge on Highway 101 was on top of the Wheeler Dam and was out in the sticks with very few people around.

She didn't know that her family rolled past her in the night while she was helping Ann prepare to survive. She heard the vehicles go by their camp and was happy that the Army didn't see them. Being captured didn't fit into her plans.

She wormed her way across the bridge as she went around stalled vehicles and wondered if anyone would eventually clear the cars from the highways or would they rust in place. She traveled several miles south of Muscle Shoals and used country roads to avoid Tuscumbia on her way to Highway 72 East.

The countryside was peaceful, and she didn't encounter any significant issues on her way to Cherokee. She went through Cherokee and saw a woman sitting on her front porch with a shotgun in her lap. Jo waved at the women and asked for directions to the FEMA camp. The woman pointed down Highway 72 West.

Jo only drove two miles before she saw Humvees and large Army trucks up ahead. She parked her truck behind an abandoned barn and walked closer to the activity. The camp was on the northwest side of the Natchez Trace Parkway and Highway 72.

She went north along the Parkway and found a clump of trees to hide in, so she could watch the camp. The camp was a mile long along the Natchez Trace Parkway and about the same depth along Highway 72. There were several rows of fences around the base and numerous guard towers. The main gate was on the Parkway and appeared to be busy. Jo watched the camp for several hours and noticed that convoys of trucks, Humvees, and other vehicles were leaving, but none was arriving.

Max and Jo took a well-deserved break as she fed him a piece of meat from last night's MRE. He ate it but then left to find his own meal. Joe opened an MRE, took a big swig of water as she saw a truck with a crane drive up to the guard tower on the far left. The crew with the truck proceeded to lower the twin .50 Cal machine guns down to a flatbed truck. The crane repeated the action three more times, and it dawned on Jo that the Army was preparing to abandon the camp.

Only a short time later, she saw soldiers bringing a large crowd of people to the gate in front of her and sending them out to the street. She observed them with her binoculars to see if her family was in the crowd. They weren't.

She saw soldiers staging thousands of people in a line that went past the back of several large trucks. The soldiers passed out water bottles and MRE boxes to the people as they passed by the trucks. The Army was releasing the prisoners, and closing the camp was the only thing that made sense.

Jo and Max walked up to the gate and looked for her family in the throngs of people as they walked out of the camp. Joe had brought one of Will's shirts and had Max stand vigil for that aroma to no avail. Over a thousand passed her, and there was no sign of any of her family

Jo started asking, "Has anyone seen Bob Karr or Jane Carter. How about Maddie O'Berg or Will Karr?"

She asked for hours until finally, she heard," I met them a couple of days ago. They left in convoy last night. They were headed to Nashville, according to one of the guards."

"Thanks so much," Jo said as she cursed under her breath.

Now it dawned on Jo that her trip was for naught; however, she didn't know if the person who told her that her family was headed to Nashville was correct. She also thought that the individual could have pulled a cruel joke on her. She stayed at the gate, checking every face in the crowd as they passed by in front of her.

She was very thankful that there were short breaks in the flow of people every time one of the large tents emptied of people. She was able to rest her eyes and eat on several occasions.

Most people appeared to be dazed and were surprised by the camp's closing. Jo talked with several groups as they stopped to decide which direction to travel. Most thought heading south gave them the best chance of survival. Many people asked her, and she pointed south. She felt terrible, but she didn't want thousands of people walking toward the Horseshoe.

The last group left the camp at 9:00 the following day, and her family wasn't in the crowd. Jo wasn't sure what had happened to them, but she hoped they were in that previous convoy and headed back to the Horseshoe. Since she had nothing to go on besides the info about the convoy, she decided to head back home.

Again, she headed south and cut across the country on dirt side roads to avoid the cities and the newly released prisoners. She crossed the river on Highway 101 and headed north to find Ann and her children. The drive up to the Highway 43 Intersection was a repeat of the other day. She dodged stalled vehicles and shot over a few groups' heads to scare them away.

Jo saw the bridge up ahead that crossed the creek where Ann and her family were hiding and drove into the woods as she had previously done before. She saw their tents up ahead, didn't see anyone around, and then checked the large tent, and it was empty. The small tent had a slight movement as she walked up to it.

She drew her pistol and said, "Ann, it's me, Jo."

She heard, "Jo, where is our momma. She left an hour ago and hasn't come back. Please find her."

"Where did she go?"

"She said she was going down to the creek and would be back in a minute. Jo, that was an hour ago."

"I'll go look for her. I want you two to load everything up and place it in the back of my truck. We'll leave as soon as your mom and I get back. Max, stay with the kids."

Jo walked down the hill to the creek and didn't see anyone. She walked down to the sandy bank and saw something that shook her. A set of footprints heading upstream mixed in with several other prints that looked like large dog paw prints. There must have been five or six of the animals following the footprints. Jo began running to find Ann before the dogs attacked.

She only ran about a hundred yards when she heard barking and growls. She slowed down and saw Ann had climbed a small tree, and she was surrounded by a pack of dogs. Owners who couldn't feed them anymore had set the poor dogs free to become wild killers.

There were too many to scare off, and they were intent on catching their prey and dining today. Even though Jo didn't want to bring attention to herself, she pulled her pistol and began shooting the dogs. She killed two when the others rushed her position. She kept her calm and shot two more when a large Rottweiler launched himself at Jo as she changed magazines. Jo ducked as a collision occurred a few inches from her face. Max had the Rottweiler by the throat, and they rolled down the hill.

Jo shot the last two dogs and could do nothing but watch Max and the massive brute fight to the death. Jo tried to get a clean shot at the Rottweiler, but the action was too fierce. The Rottweiler yelped then fell silent. Max limped over to Jo and rested his head on her foot.

Jo rubbed his ears and said, "Good Max. Good dog."

Ann climbed down from the tree and was very thankful that Jo and Max had saved her from a terrible fate. Jo checked Max and found several puncture wounds from bites but nothing severe. They walked back to the truck and found everything loaded and ready to go. Joe made room for Max in back, and he jumped up and lay down in his new bed. Jo rubbed some antibiotics on his wounds, and they left the camp.

They had driven for several hours before Jo decided to make camp just before the Highway 840 and Highway 102 junction. She pulled off the road and had to use wire cutters to cut the fence to hide the truck in a stand of trees. She was careful to make sure no one saw her pull off into the trees and then walked up to the highway and stood guard while Ann pitched the tents.

Max began acting odd and wanted her to follow him back to the camp when she heard the truck's motor roar to life. The truck came flying out of the woods about fifty yards east of her, broke through the fence and never slowed down as it headed east on Highway 840. Jo led Max down to where the camp had been and found her backpack with a note attached.

The note said: **Thanks for all of you help, but I need your truck more than you do. Good Luck. Ann**

"That rotten bitch stole Bob's truck. May her sorry ass rot in hell," Jo yelled.

Max looked concerned and laid his head in Jo's lap as she ranted and raved about never helping anyone ever again.

It was about an hour before dark, so Jo decided to go ahead and spend the night in the area; however, she walked back into the woods to a subdivision to find an empty house. She watched the neighborhood for a while and didn't see anyone stirring around. She skipped the community for a beautiful farmhouse across a side street east of the houses.

The house was abandoned quickly and had not been searched. There was rotting food on the table and food in the dead refrigerator. She also found plenty of can goods in the pantry and home canned food on shelves in the basement. Max and Jo ate very well that night.

Jo woke up early the following day and tried to open a gun safe in the basement but gave up after twisting the combination knob numerous times. Max wanted to go outside, and she saw him sniffing around a pole barn in the backyard. She pushed the sliding door open and immediately became sick to her stomach. The house owners were holding each other in death as they had held each other for over fifty years. The 1959 Corvette had run out of gas as it supplied the fumes to give the couple the peace they sought in each other's arms. They decided to choose the death they wanted rather than face the apocalypse.

Jo left them alone other than placing a tarp over their rotting bodies. What interested her most was a 1968 short bed 4x4 sitting next to the Corvette. The truck had been restored and was in pristine condition. Jo fired it up and took it out of the pole barn and out into the fresh air. She went back into the house and brought out all of the can goods and most of the home canned goods. She filled several Mason jars with water and took them to the truck.

On a whim, she held her breath, dug the man's wallet out of his back pocket, and searched it for the combination. Sure enough, it was written on the back of his wife's photo.

The safe opened, and there was a treasure of guns and ammunition. Jo also saw several cigar boxes and opened one to find it full of silver coins. All six of the boxes contained gold or silver coins. Jo decided to leave them.

There were only one AR and a couple of Berettas. The rest were cowboy six shooters and lever action Winchesters in several calibers and a couple of shotguns. The real find was 1,000 rounds of .223 and 2,000 rounds of 9mm along with several thousand rounds of several different calibers. Jo took one of the 12 Gauge pumps to the barn, found a saw, cut the barrel down, and cut off the stock. She loaded it with buckshot and made a sling so she could wear it across her shoulder.

Jo took them all to the truck and placed the guns in the cab and ammo under a tarp with the food and water. She searched the house one more time and changed her mind about the silver and gold. The people were dead, and the gold and silver might be needed to help her family one day. She stuffed the boxes under the truck's seat and knew it was time to hit the road.

Jo continued what had become her regular routine of ducking around wrecks and stalled cars between bouts of scaring assholes away from her truck. She'd only been on the road for half an hour when she saw Bob's old truck crashed into the back of a semi-trailer. The cab was full of holes, and the glass was broken. Jo carefully searched the area and found the four bodies on the side of the road. The kids had been shot in the head, and Ann was naked and lay on the hood of a car.

The truck had been stripped of everything usable, and there was no sign of the people who had valued the kid's lives so little. Jo got back in the truck and was much more careful as she passed people on the road.

She took the backroads around Lebanon again and arrived at the bridge to Hartsville again. She dreaded dodging the roadblocks and the corrupt police force one more time. She inched her way up the bridge and didn't see any barrier. She drove toward town before taking a side road and went north to go around the city. She didn't see anyone for several miles until she crossed Highway 25, and there was a steady stream of people heading toward Dixon Springs.

She went north, caught a side road, and headed east until she was above the city. She took Young Branch Road down to the town and had to shoot several times to run thugs away from her truck. She crossed Highway 25 and saw a crowd of people gathered by the Post Office and had a dreadful feeling. She hoped no one recognized her as she pulled closer.

That thought flew out of her head as a woman yelled, "That's the bitch that killed Dave and Fred. Get her."

Jo stopped the truck, leveled the shotgun at the crowd, and pumped six shots of buckshot into them. She pitched the shotgun into the bed, jumped into the truck and sped off toward the Horseshoe knocking people out of the way, as the engine roared. Several bullets struck the back of the truck, but none hit Jo or Max.

Jo stopped in front of the gate, saw Jack, and yelled, "Let me in before those bastards kill me."

She drove the truck past the gate and said, "Jack, I couldn't find my family, but I think they might be in Nashville."

"Jo, they arrived here just a while ago. They are all okay and thinking about sending out a search party to find you."

"Oh thank God they are okay. I'm going back home to my family. And they are all okay?"

"Yes. Will got a bump on the head, but Maddie is taking good care of him. Jane, Maddie, and Will are at Bob's."

"Don't radio Bob or anyone. I want to surprise them."

Jo drove the short trip down to Bob's place and parked the bright red truck in front of the house. Before she could get out of the house, Bob and Bill came out to see who was visiting.

Bill saw his wife and yelled, "Jo, you're back. We were scared that you had been captured."

"I went to the camp, and they were all gone. We can swap stories later, kiss me, and take me to my kids."

"Jo, my black truck has turned red and gotten twenty years younger. Did you have trouble?"

"I'll fill you in later, but the short story is I saved the lives of a woman and her two kids, and she repaid me by stealing your truck."

"Don't worry about the truck. Come on in the house. Missy and Jake are in the house. Maddie and Will are in the trailer. Will is still recuperating from a bump on his head."

"Mama, Mama, you're back. I was so worried about you," said Missy as she wrapped her arms around her mother.

Jake ran up and knocked both of them to the floor as he piled into the group hug. Jane came from the kitchen and waved at Jo as she wallowed on the floor with Missy and Jake.

"Jo thanks for coming to rescue us, but thanks to the Major we were set free and brought back home. It's a long story, and we'll compare notes after the town meeting tonight. Why don't you get cleaned up before supper and we'll all go to the town meeting this evening."

"I think I'd rather stay home with my family."

"Bill spoke up and said, "This is a critical meeting. We were almost wiped out by Walkers this morning and have to set some folks straight on their duties and responsibilities. They almost got us all killed."

"Okay, but first I need to go out to see Will."

"He's out in the trailer. Knock first," Missy said."

Jo said, "What," and then proceeded quickly out to the trailer with Jane following.

"Jo, hold on. Those two love each other and please don't be heavy handed with them."

"How close have they gotten?"

"Jo, to keep the family together we all had to tell the guards that we were married. They've been sleeping on a single bunk bed for several days half-naked. You can hear every move someone makes when everyone is only three feet apart from the next bunk. The Lord only knows what went on below those covers and Jo; I hope they did find love. Hell Bob and I did several times."

"Mom, that's TMI about you and Bob having sex. My question is can Maddie be pregnant."

"I don't think so, but that's not the worst that could happen to a couple madly in love during an apocalypse."

She didn't knock and slowly opened the door to see Will and Maddie on the couch. Will was lying down with his head on Maddie's lap. He was asleep, and Maddie was caressing his hair as she read a magazine.

Jo whispered, "Maddie, don't wake him up."

Maddie was surprised and replied, "Momma Jo, we missed you so much and were worried sick about you.

Joe hugged Maddie, and then pulled a chair up beside her as she said, "How is our young man doing?"

"He's okay, but it scared me to death. A guard hit him because he was protecting me from another guard. He is my hero."

"Maddie, I hate to pry into your business, but what is your and Will's relationship? Do you love him?"

"Will is my boyfriend, and I love him. He told me he loved me days ago, but it took me a bit longer to know exactly how I felt about him. I can't imagine life without him now."

"Have y'all taken precaution?"

Maddie almost choked and replied, "We didn't do anything that would get me pregnant."

"That didn't answer my question."

"Mamma Jo, I love your son, and that's all you need to know. What we do in bed is our business."

"I'm sorry. You are right. I can't treat Will like a child anymore. I'm sorry."

Maddie hugged Jo and said, "You've had Will for 17 years and did a good job raising him. He's a man now, and I will take care of him from now on. I love him."

"You love him, but are you ready to live with him the rest of your life?"

"Yes."

"Then we will have a wedding as soon as possible. My grandkids will be born to a married mom and dad."

Will opened his eyes and said, "I heard every word, and yes I want to marry Maddie. That is if you two let me have a say in the matter."

Jo kissed Will on the forehead and then pinched him as she said, "I know you've been sleeping with this hussy at the FEMA camp and you have to make an honest woman out of her. Besides, I've been planning a wedding since you two met. Now put some damn clothes on and no practicing until after the wedding."

They were all around the table by 6:00 pm, and Bob said grace as usual. He gave special thanks for everyone returning safely and asked God to bless their leaders with the wisdom to see them through the days ahead. He introduced Helen and Gabby to everyone and then announced that one of the deacons from the church was an ordained preacher and that he would be conducting Bob and Jane's wedding next Saturday.

Jo added, "I think we should have a double wedding that day. Will has proposed to Maddie, and she wants to officially join our family."

Bill raised his glass and said, "Here's a toast to our happy couples and may they live happily ever after."

Bob reminded everyone it was time to go to Greg's for the meeting. The evening was cool and the drive short; they arrived a few minutes early, and the place was packed. Everyone but the guards pulling their shifts was present.

Greg started to call the group to attention when Bob waved him off, banged the butt of his pistol on the table, and said, "It's time for the meeting to start. Pipe down and listen. As most of you know, I just returned from being captured by some FEMA goons but was released by Major Payne and his team."

Bob had introduced the Major, his daughter and his team before proceeding.

"Now to the issue, I've begun an investigation into the alleged misconduct of some of our team at the gate over the past few days.

Mr. Grinnell interrupted and said, "Those are facts, not allegations. The massacre did happen. I saw it with my own eyes."

"Sit down and shut up. The misdeeds are the dereliction of duty by Grinnell, Nelson and three of the guards on duty. All five of you were cowards and shirked your responsibility to guard the Horseshoe against invaders. The second issue is the six men and women who did not come to help fight off the invading force this afternoon. Had we not arrived all of you would be dead or slaves.

Grinnell, Nelson and the three guards are now under arrest and will leave the Horseshoe by noon tomorrow. I should have you lined up and shot for cowardice and treason. Idiots there are no innocent people out there. Your cowardice resulted in seven wounded and one dead from our community.

Nelson charged Bob and Bob sidestepped, knocked him down, and stuck the barrel of his .45 to Nelson's head.

"Anyone else tries that shit, and I'll shoot instead of knocking your ass to the ground."

"Most of the group applauded, but a small handful were outraged."

Debbie Green stood up and said, "This is a democracy, and you can't do that to people."

"No, you elected me dictator for 30 days to do exactly what I'm doing to save your asses from idiots like Nelson who will get you all killed. The people who are trying to get us killed are the outsiders from Dixon Springs. That excludes Jack and his family. If you outsiders don't want to be here or give your food away, we will evict you from the Horseshoe with a week's supply of food, and you can do what you want with it.

The six who didn't come to help fight will receive the punishment to be decided by six of the original residents of the Horseshoe. Anyone who doesn't fight in the future will be evicted if I don't shoot them first. Not fighting to protect your friends and family deserves the death penalty."

"Mrs. Green asked, "What if you don't believe in killing?"

"That's your choice, but if you don't fight, get the hell out of here before I shoot your sorry ass. Look, I don't want to be a hard ass but the world you know has ended. Those typically great people want to kill you for your food."

The Major spoke up, "Bob can I address the community?"

"Yes."

"Bob is right about the need to stand and fight for your community and its possessions. There are about 200 million starving people out walking from town to town scavenging for food. It's going to get worse. Disease, gangs, and medicine running out will contribute to the death toll and violence. My team is starting a community like yours a few miles north of here, and Jim Dickerson is starting a third community on the west side of the river. We plan to band together to help each other survive and perhaps help keep civilization alive."

Mrs. Green stated, "But the government will come and help us."

The Major responded, "No they won't. They shut down all operations from the east coast to the west coast. Only California and the North East are receiving help from the government. It's horrible, but it's the truth. I was ordered to disband the FEMA camp I was in charge of along with the others in the middle of the USA. We are on our own and need to be strong, or we'll get run over."

Greg spoke up, "I failed you this morning by interfering with Jack's orders to shoot the attackers. I apologize for my mistake and won't blame you if I am also punished."

Bob looked Greg in the eye and said, "Yes you will be punished with a double workload for the next thirty days. I think you learned from your mistake."

The meeting went on for another half hour, and Bob told the council to meet at his house in the morning at 8:00 am sharp.

"Ben, please join us at this meeting. We'll also feed your team.

***

Jo, Bill, Bob, and Jane sat on the back deck winding down from the hectic day's events with a bottle of Bulleit and conversation.

"Jo, do you think Maddie would be okay with a double wedding?"

"I think she would be all right with that. I don't know who she'll want to give her away."

"Damn, I don't have anyone to give me away to Bob. I think I'll ask Will to do the honor," said Jane.

"Dad, I'll be your best man, and you can be Will's."

"Bill, you should be your son's best man, and he can be mine or hell you can be best man for both of us."

Jo changed the subject and said, "Jane, what do you think of Maddie?"

"I like her and have claimed her as a second daughter."

"Well, that's icky. Will's marrying his aunt."

"That's an honorary daughter. We're from Kentucky, not West Virginia," Jane laughed as she replied.

"Now what do you really think about her. Is she a good fit for Will and the family?"

Bob answered before anyone could open their mouths, "They fit pretty good together on that bunk all spooned up together every night."

"Pop, you have a dirty mind and besides mom told me that you two were doing more than holding hands."

"No, I have a clean mind and know all about the birds and bees. What I do know is that they have only known each other for ten days and have been together every minute of every day and been through more together than most people in a year. I also know that if they don't get married, soon she might end up knocked up."

Bill laughed and said, "Dad, you never candy coat anything do you?"

"Bill I told your mom the same thing about you and Jo..."

"Pop, shut up while you are still on my good side. You do know that she is Senator O'Berg's daughter," Jo said.

"Jane and I have known for a couple of days. Does that change your opinion of her," replied Bob.

"Do what," replied Bill, and then he added, "How can such a sweet young girl be related to that scumbag?"

"Hold on. Jo, go get Maddie and Will and let's see what she has to say about her dad."

Jo went to the camper and invited the two lovebirds out to the deck for drinks and warned Maddie that the topic of her father had come up.

"My mom was a young dumb country girl when he took advantage of her. We both hate the bastard, and I haven't seen him in years. Please don't judge me on his actions," replied Maddie as she walked up to Jane, stole her whiskey, and downed it in one swallow.

"Slow down girl, good whiskey is meant to be enjoyed not slammed," Bob said.

"Papaw Bob, I'm sorry, but I don't want to be judged by that asshole."

"Calm down Maddie," said Jane as she pulled Maddie onto her lap and said, "We love you, and you are part of our family. I knew when I first saw you laying there with Will's hand on your boob that you and Will would get married. I want you to always think of me as a second mother."

"So Will was feeling me up as I lay there unconscious?"

Will stammered and said, "I was asleep."

"Don't worry Jo. Will is a perfect gentleman, well most of the time," Maddie replied.

Will asked, "What are we going to do about sleeping arrangements when we all get married. The kids have to go."

Jo said, "We'll figure that out tomorrow. You two need to sleep in your own beds until then."

Bob laughed and replied, "Good luck on that."

Will laughed and said, "Dad, Mom, what is the new drinking age? I've been drinking your beer for several years, and that whiskey looks pretty good. I can serve in our army and get shot. I should be able to get a shot."

Bob poured a little whiskey in two glasses, passed them to Will and Maddie, and said, "Welcome to the Apocalypse. May you live long enough to enjoy each other forever after."

Jo bumped her glass against Will and Maddie's glasses and said, "I'm not losing a son, I'm gaining a warrior daughter."

They stayed up until midnight recounting their adventures and Bob told the story about the guard grabbing Maddie's ass and Will stomping the guard several times.

*

Chapter 7

Day 10 – Neighbors Attacking.

As usual, Jane woke up before the others and put a pot of coffee on while she put her makeup on for the day. She looked in the mirror, saw a beautiful dark haired woman who seemed much young than her actual age, and said, "Damn, you're too good for the likes of Bob Karr."

"I can hear you."

"Bob, I'm only going to wear makeup for special occasions from this day on to stretch my supply out as long as possible."

"Have I ever seen you without makeup? Will I run screaming?"

"Smart ass."

"I don't see your ass doing any tricks," Bob replied.

"That's not what you said last night."

"Mom, what kind of tricks were you doing last night?" Maddie said as she poured her and Will a cup of coffee."

"Grandma you can pass on answering that," Will said as he sat down at the kitchen table."

"Maddie replied, "How am I going to learn to please my man if I don't learn from a more experienced woman."

Bob was tongue tied but finally said, "Got to change the damn locks to keep the undesirable's out of the house. How did you two do sleeping in your own beds last night?"

"We went to bed in our own beds as requested. I got cold a few minutes later and had to rub my cold butt...err...feet on Will to get warm."

"Ah the good intentions of men pave the road to hell,' said Bob.

Will countered with, "Or heaven as the case may be."

"Let's change the subject. Maddie, who do you want to walk you down the aisle at the wedding?"

"Mom, I know this may be weird, but I want you to give me away to Will."

"Jane grinned from ear to ear and replied, "I would be deeply honored young lady. We will start a new post-apocalyptic tradition."

"Thanks, Mom."

"Papaw, I'm going to ask Dad to be my best man. I want you, but it would be best if dad did the honor."

"I agree son."

"Maddie, we have to get together and discuss wedding gowns and such. I'm not sure we'll have much choice, but we need to do the best we can," said Jane.

"Will, I have several suits that we can wear. Yours will be a bit large but not too big for you."

Jo and Bill came to the kitchen next followed by Missy. They poured a cup of sunshine to get their eyes functioning and joined in the lively conversation about the wedding, where Maddie slept last night, and what the drinking age should be. Jo's vote was one year older than Missy was every year.

"Mom, Will, and I have been drinking your beer and wine for years. I've never been drunk and can't stand being out of control. You can trust me."

Will added, "Missy when are you going to introduce Izzy's son, Matt, to Mom and Dad?"

"Matt's kinda shy,' but he is a real nice guy. We've been in Grandma's classes together, and I think he is my boyfriend."

"What is Izzy's last name?"

Everyone looked around the table, and only Missy knew the answer.

"Dad, it's Izzy."

"I know his name is Izzy, but what is his last name?"

His last name is Izzy. His first name actually is Marion."

"What kind of last name is Izzy?"

"His great grandfather couldn't read or write when he landed at Ellis Island back in the 1890's and couldn't spell the family name, which was Iskandrian, so the clerk wrote Izzy, and it stuck."

Bob replied, "Thank God their name wasn't ...."

"Shut up Bob," replied Jo, "we have young ears at the table.

"Mom, I'll be 16 in two months. I'm almost an old maid."

"Missy, does Izzy have a wife?" Jo asked.

"No. She died in a car wreck a few years back.

"Then we need to introduce Helen to him," Joe replied.

Bob said, "Women can't stand a single woman mingling among their men. And that young lady is a good looking filly."

Maddie reached over, gave Jo a high five, and said, "Mamma Jo, I have so much to learn about life from you and Mamma Jane."

Jane slapped Bob on the head and said, "I'm the only filly that you should be looking at."

The others started filtering in, so Bob took the council members outside to the picnic table to allow Jane, Jo, and Maddie to prepare breakfast.

Ben started by asking, "Could we set up a meeting with Jim Dickerson ASAP?

Bob replied, "Yes, I'll send someone over with a message after breakfast."

"No need. We have these," Ben said as he showed them a fancy walkie-talkie. These reach 25 miles and on a good day 30 miles. This one is for you Bob. Jim has one also."

"Well, that makes things easier. Now let's get a couple of things out of the way.

Greg, choose six people to decide on the punishment for the six who balked at fighting. If they don't agree to defend our community, they must be banished."

Everyone agreed, so they moved on to a few other quick topics before the food arrived.

"We need to establish more rules for Betty Lou to add to our charter. They are:

1. The law on the age to drink.

2. The age of consent.

3. The legal age to marry without parental permission?

4. What age does consensual sex become child rape?

5. Is there a retirement age?

That's all I can remember from lying awake last night."

Will said, "I know where several of those came from and I have some input."

Greg replied, "We need to hear all sides of the argument."

"In my opinion, the drinking age and age to get married without parental consent should be the same. I would suggest 16. I know we will ask 12-year-olds to fight and die for the community, but that's only in extreme situations. Alcohol and drugs will always be a problem and any laws should have harsh punishment for breaking laws while under the influence."

Betty Lou said, "That's very thoughtful Will. If every young adult were as mature as you, we wouldn't need these laws, but unfortunately, we will run into these problems. The one that bothers me is the age of consent. We all know when we started having sex behind the barn or in the car at the drive inn. I just don't want a sixteen year old going to jail for consensual sex with a 14 or 15-year-old."

Bob said, "If the age of consent is 15, then a 40-year-old can have sex with a 15-year old or marry them for that matter."

Betty Lou replied, "Yep, we'd better think this through or all of these old men will be marrying 13-year-olds like Jerry Lee Lewis did back in the 1950's."

"That was his cousin to boot."

Will asked, "Who the heck is Mr. Lewis?

The food came, and the council ate while debating these thought provoking issues. Joe, Maddie, and Jane joined the conversation, and it became much livelier. Maddie and Jo were two very opinionated women and brought some differing views to the conversation that ended with all of the new rules being tabled for the entire communities input.

Maddie brought up a new one, "Bob, will abortions be allowed in our community. I for one think they should be illegal."

"I'll kick that one down the road to the long-term leader of the community. I personally think that assuming the USA loses only 70% of its population, we will need every baby born just for mankind to survive. I'll let the community figure that one out. Now moving along, Ben, when and where will we meet with Dickerson and his group?"

"They should be on this side of the river now. Could you send someone to pick them up by the cabins?"

"Jack, could you take my truck and pick up our guests?"

"I'll be glad to."

Jim, Hoss and Steve Alford were brought back to Bob's house, and after introductions, the talks began by placing a map in front of the team.

Ben pointed to the three communities and said, "Jim's group covers over two hundred square miles from the Horseshoe to this side of Lebanon and has about 200 people. You all know the Horseshoe. My community includes the land east of Lafayette and North of Lebanon. We have over 100 families that want to join us."

Bob asked, "What are the known threats to Jim and your communities?"

"Senator O'Berg has started a dictatorship in Lebanon and is trying to expand his empire. He has put Jim on notice that his people have to pay taxes to live in his little country. My area only has O'Berg to the south and a few drug gangs in Lafayette to contend with right now. The immediate threats to us all are the people flooding into the area from Nashville and the large northern cities. I arrived yesterday in the middle of a situation that could have gone either way."

"Will asked, "Major, what should we be doing to prevent the Walkers from overrunning the Horseshoe?"

"Keep doing what you've been doing but get everyone on board with eliminating any threats. You also need to find ways to stop the threats without expending valuable ammunition. You might try ditches with diesel fuel, flamethrowers, snares, and poison. Save as many bullets as possible."

Maddie responded with, "Bows and arrows. We can get the arrows back and reuse them."

"Great idea."

Jack added, "It's been a full-time job burying the hundreds of bodies that have stacked up just in the past few days. We're taking them out of the Horseshoe and burying them in trenches over by the old reactor."

"That's what I'd do. Bury them before rats spread disease."

Ben said, "Now moving on, I propose that we institute a council made up of an equal number of people from each group, and they can select a chairman to conduct the meetings but does not have any authority over the group."

They all agreed, and Ben was selected to be the interim chairman.

"Now, I'd like to close the meeting and have a meeting with just the leaders of the three communities."

The rest of the group left, and Ben looked Jim and Bob in the eyes and said, "Gentlemen we are at war with O'Berg and his henchmen. We need a plan to defeat them, and we must accomplish that task quickly. My sources tell me that approximately a month from now FEMA is sending men, weapons, and supplies to support O'Berg who they think is the elected leader of the area."

"That would tip the balance of power in his favor, and we might not ever regain control of our communities," said Jim.

Bob replied, "We have several options. We can take out O'Berg, take out his entire team, capture the convoy bringing the men and supplies, or move from the area and start a new community."

Jim said, "My team has identified the community leaders who support O'Berg and O'Berg's, henchmen. My vote is to start a guerilla action to cut the head off the snake and end the threat before it gets stronger. We need your Wraith to focus his efforts on the Senator."

Ben came to attention and asked, "Who is the Wraith?"

Bob replied, "Someone has been killing gang members, outlaws and thugs in the area around the Horseshoe and whoever he is, he leaves his signature. The Wraith. The people outside the Horseshoe think it's someone from our group. I'm not convinced that's accurate; however, we could use about twenty Wraiths to clean up Lebanon."

Ben replied, "I'd like each team to give me four volunteers with military experience to start a hit squad to take out the Senator and his loyal followers."

They all agreed to supply people for the hit squad, and Bob began to wonder whom he could get to volunteer. He only had a few ex-military in his group, but he did have several who were excellent snipers.

Jim replied, "The top four are O'Berg, Walt Long, Fred Ham, and Bill Middleton. I'll get a list and location of the next level below those four."

"Wait a minute; Jo had a partner named Walt Long on the Louisville police force," answered Bob.

"It has to be the same asshole. This guy was a cop in Louisville, and he came south looking for his girlfriend."

"Shit that sounds like Jo's partner. I'll check with her," replied Bob.

***

"Pop, that almost has to be my partner from Louisville. Jim says he has turned evil?"

"Yes, he has taken over the police force and has ruthlessly killed anyone who speaks out against the Senator."

"Walt was odd and a pain in the ass, but I never thought he'd go rogue and start killing people," replied Jo.

Bill spoke up, "It doesn't surprise me at all. I always thought he was an explosion waiting to happen. Jo, I wasn't going to tell you this, but I caught him holding your hand in the hospital when you were unconscious."

"Bill, don't be jealous. We were partners."

"No that's not it. When I confronted him, he basically said that he could take better care of you than I could and threatened to take you away from me. He is obsessed with you. I think you are the girlfriend that he is looking for."

"Oh shit, I think you are right. That last day he flipped out when I told him that I was going to report him if he didn't stop flirting with me. He probably went off the deep end. Bill, he might try to kill you!"

"I'll kill him first."

Jo looked at Bill and said, "I believe you would."

Jo saw Izzy and took Helen over to meet him.

"Helen this is Izzy, he is a dear friend and a great person. Izzy this is Helen. She was lost, and we brought her here to live with us. Izzy, Bob wants you to show Helen and her daughter Gabby around the Horseshoe."

Izzy and Helen left and caught each other up on the past two weeks while Maddie and Jo finished their last cup of coffee. They chatted just like old friends as he led her around the Horseshoe.

"Well mom, that takes care of Helen. We will probably have to throw a little gas on their romance fire, but the twinkle in his eyes told me he will fall for her."

"I feel the same about her liking him. Mission accomplished."

***

Ben wouldn't accept Maddie or Jane to be on the hit squad, and it royally pissed Maddie off.

"Momma-Jane, I know that I don't have a lot of experience, but I can learn quickly and want to rid this country of these assholes."

"Darling you can call me Jane now if you want to. Darling, the killing is easy. It's trying to forget killing that eats away at you the rest of your life. Don't start unless you are strong enough to block the shit from your mind afterward. You love Will and want to marry him. What will the poor boy do if you get killed in a raid?"

"Mom, I don't want to kill people. I hope no one wants to kill people, but Will and I want to have three kids and raise them in a safe, loving environment. We can't do that if these thugs rule the world. Can you train me Miss Wraith?"

"How long have you known?"

"Since I saw you come back in late that morning. How do you slip away from Bob without him missing you?"

She laughed and replied, "I take him to bed and let's just say that when I'm done with him, he sleeps like a baby too worn out to get up in the night."

Maddie blushed and said, "So there are other perks to getting rid of assholes."

"We'll begin your training this evening after work is done. Let's train Will and Missy at the same time, so Will won't wonder why we keep slipping off to the shooting range and training area."

Will and Maddie were assigned to guard duty now that the wall and fence had been constructed. Will was on horseback patrolling the east river bank while Maddie manned the east side guard tower. They waved at each other when Will rode near the top of the Horseshoe by the wall. Will always blew her a kiss, which she faithfully returned.

Will saw Hoss and Jim on their side of the river throwing three large bundles in the river and then they waved and drove off in Jim's old truck. Will knew they had taken out some trash and threw the weighted bodies in the river. He thought for a minute and made a note to never drink from the river without using a LifeStraw.

Will's replacement showed up at 4:00, and it was time to pick Maddie up at the tower. He galloped north to the building when he heard gunfire from up ahead and urged his horse to run faster to where Maddie was located.

He arrived just as another shot rang out from the tower. He looked and couldn't see what Maddie was shooting at. A minute later, she climbed down from the tower with her .338 Lapua chambered rifle on her shoulder.

He kissed her and said, "Babe, what were you shooting at?"

There were some biker scumbags trying to rob a couple across the river. I nailed two, and the rest took off like the scared scumbags they are."

"Damn, how far away were they?"

"I don't know for sure; they were past the range finder's capacity. I guessed it was 850-900 yards and aimed a bit high. I got the first one in the ass, adjusted, and got the next one in the chest. The farmer finished off the first one and waved back at me."

"Darn, you're getting good with that rifle."

"Papaw Bob has really helped me with my accuracy. Now the training with Momma Jane will help make me a real expert sniper."

Will took her in his arms, kissed her, and said, "My baby the avenging angel."

"What does that mean?"

"Baby, Papaw, and I also know that Grandma is the Wraith. We guessed Grandma would intensify your training. Papaw will be speaking to her tonight on how we can help y'all get rid of the scum without getting your cute little asses shot to pieces."

"Jane thinks Bob doesn't have a clue."

"Baby, Papaw Bob was just happy as hell with her method of making him sleep all night."

"So you know what I was going to do to wear you out?"

"Papaw is a gentleman and kept the details to himself; however my imagination has been running wild."

"Why you little shit. Just for that, I'll just slip you a sleeping pill."

"Unh-unh, I want to full treatment," he said as he pulled her close and kissed her.

Missy was pleased that their Grandma would give them the much-needed training and joined in enthusiastically. Jane gave all of them gun safety, proper shooting techniques, and plenty of range time the first day. It was fun shooting the Stoeger high-powered pellet guns but not as fulfilling as firing the real weapons but saved ammunition.

The training went on for several days as Jane went on to cover knife fighting, camouflage, infiltration/exfiltration, and a hundred ways to kill with your bare hands. Missy and Will had taken Jujitsu classes, and both were ahead of Maddie on hand to hand fighting.

They were riding in an ATV back home when there was a loud bang from a bullet ricocheting off the ATV's frame. The bullet disintegrated, and several pieces hit Will and Maddie on their backs. The bullet strike was closely followed by the sound of a gunshot from across the river.

Jane gunned the motor and drove behind a slight rise to block the sniper's view.

Jane said, "Is everyone okay?"

"Maddie and I were hit by fragments. I'm okay, let me check Maddie's back."

Maddie pulled her shirt over her head exposed her back, and Will saw two wounds with the fragments still on top of the flesh. Will picked them out using his knife while Jane handed him two bandages from the first aid kit.

"Her wounds aren't serious and have already stopped bleeding, I'm going to kill the bastards that hurt my girl," Will exclaimed.

There was a steady drone of gunfire from across the river from close and far away.

"I think they are trying to soften us up before they try to invade again. Maddie, get your .338 and follow me to the far end of the rise," said Jane.

As they crawled to the end of the rise to get an excellent position to return fire, they heard return fire from the guards and people inside the Horseshoe. They crawled to the end, and Jane used her binoculars to spot the snipers on the far side of the river.

"Maddie, see the tall oak tree about a hundred yards left of the barn. There is a man about half way up the tree and two more on top of the barn. The range is about 750 yards. Adjust your rifle and try to hit all three. Will, your .223 probably won't be accurate enough, but I want you to shoot the man on the left side of the roof on the barn. Get ready."

Will's AR had a 3x9 power scope and he quickly figured out which cross bar on the reticle to place on the target, Maddie's rifle was sighted in for 900 yards, so she just had to check for windage to be ready.

Jane said, "The wind is very mild but is blowing right to left. Aim slightly left of dead center and pray. Ready, shoot."

They took a deep breath, kept the reticle on target, and squeezed the triggers with the ball of their fingers. Both guns fired simultaneously, and Maddie's man fell out of the tree. Will's bullet hit the roof to the left of the man, so he adjusted and fired again. The man rolled from the roof followed by the man next to him after Maddie's .338 tore his heart to pieces.

Jane scanned the far side of the river and found two more snipers hiding on top of an old oil tank about 500 yards away and pointed them out to Will and Maddie.

"I'll get the one on the left. You nail the other one," Will said.

"Bet you a big kiss I get mine with one shot, "Maddie replied.

Will took aim and fired when Jane gave the signal. Maddie fired at the same time, and both men fell from the tank.

Jane scanned the other side for a few minutes and said, "I can't find anymore. Let's head on down to the house and check to see if everyone's okay and make sure there are no snipers shooting at our family."

"Grandma, we have to get more radios. I'll bet the news of the attack didn't spread quickly enough to avoid casualties."

"Son, you hit the nail on the head. We have to be able to react and send our people to the hot spots much quicker."

They drove on to Bob's house, and during the short drive, they were shot at several times from long range across the river. Jane didn't stop because she was worried about her family. They pulled into the driveway under heavy fire and dove for cover. The sons of a bitches were targeting Bob's house in hopes of killing the leader of the Horseshoe.

They crawled to the side of the house and found that the house blocked the bullets. Jane, Will, and Maddie climbed up an old TV antenna tower beside the house and joined Bob and Jo on top of the roof.

Bob yelled, "The bastards are across the river lobbing bullets at us. Most of the rounds are puny assed .22 Long Rife or several of us would be dead. He pointed to a wound on his back. Poor little Jake got hit on the foot. He'll be okay the bullets were spent by the time they hit us. Be careful because they do have at least a couple of deer rifles."

Jane replied, "I only see three roof tops and the bridge where the shots could be originating from. The .22 shots are poke and hope."

A bullet hit between Will and Maddie, and then they heard the rifle report from behind them. Will and Maddie both spun around aimed and shot the two men on top of Bob's barn.

"Pop, they had a damn forward observer. Pardon my French," Maddie yelled as the men tumbled from the roof.

Jane laughed and said, "Bob and I speak fluent French. Good shots."

"Will added, "I'll bet we just got a new radio tuned to their frequency. I'm going to redirect their fire."

Will scrambled down from the house, ran over to the dead men, and found the radio. He scanned the area around him, placed his handkerchief over the mic, and said. Aim a little to the left you're drifting away from the house."

"Will do. Have they spotted you yet?"

"Hell no. I shot one of the women and almost hit Karr. He's been wounded, and they drug his sorry ass into the house."

The bullet strikes drifted slowly to their left as Will had directed. This gave Jane and Maddie the ability to focus on the houses across the river, and they found the bastards and began to eliminate them one by one, as Bob kept firing on the ones to the south. The targets were from 950 to 1,150 yards away, and only Maddie had the longer range .338 to get first shot kills. Bob and Jane's 30-06 had the stopping power at that range, their scopes were low quality, and they hit their target about every third shot.

Even with those issues, all of the long-range shooters were eliminated in about 15 minutes, and then they started looking for the assholes lobbing the .22s at them.

Jo yelled, "Hey, look to the left of the bridge across the creek by the old welding shop. There is a small crowd with rifles pointing up to the sky."

Bob aimed his more powerful binoculars in that direction. He saw the people shooting and said, "The bastards have to aim for the sky to lob those puny bullets at us. Everyone set up for about 1,100 yards, and we'll bombard their asses. Maddie, you can aim directly at them the rest of us will aim high and let the bullets fly. Will and Jo, shoot a whole magazine at them without stopping. We will scare the hell out of them if nothing else. I'll spot and direct your fire. Maddie, you are own your own."

They all made their best guess on elevation and began to fire on their unsuspecting target. Maddie's first .338 took out the window of a car behind them killing two people in the car. She saw the window shatter and adjust elevation and began picking off the bastards before they realized they were dropping like flies. Jo and Will fired their 30 rounds, shoved another 30 round magazine in, and kept firing randomly at the area. Jane fired the 30-06 with some accuracy and hit a few of her targets.

The gunfire from the other side stopped, and all hell broke loose on the sorry assed people shooting at their neighbors. Twenty of the large group lay dying as their friends lost their courage and ran like the rats they were. The odd thing was that most of these folks were from the area and had primarily been law-abiding people until the food ran out.

Mother's saw their twelve-year-old son's dying in the parking lot beside their Marlin and Ruger.22 LR Rifles. Husbands died beside their son's trying to kill their neighbors to take their food. The worst part was that Bob and his family would row across the river in an hour, see the carnage, and cry for the men, women, and children who died trying to kill them.

Maddie finally understood what Jane had meant about being able to live with the killing.

Bob radioed Jack and found out that Jack and Ben took a raiding party over to the other side and were engaged in a running gun battle with the attacking force.

"Bob we have the two Humvees, and Ben's team is ripping them up any time they stop to fight, or we corner them. We are systematically wiping them out. We will miss some because about a third of them threw down their guns and went back to their houses. We'll have to develop a plan for them."

"Thanks for the update."

Bob, Bill, Will, and Maddie left in Bob's truck to visit the rest of their team to see how they fared in the fight. Bill brought first aid supplies to treat any of the wounded.

Their first stop was Greg's place, and they found a large part of their team gathered there licking their wounds. Betty Lou suffered the most series wound and would recover from the small caliber wound to her leg. Bill had to dig deep to extract the bullet from her upper thigh. She would be sore for a couple of weeks but would soon be back to full strength.

They went on stopping to check for wounded, and Bill patched up any they encountered. When they got to the wall, they saw Izzy holding one of the guards in his arms. She was his sister, Kathy, and she had been struck in the chest by a high-powered bullet and died quickly.

Izzy was weeping with Helen trying to console him.

Izzy looked up, saw Bob, and said, "She has no husband, and her daughter is only ten years old. I will raise her as my own and tell her every day what a beautiful person her mother was."

Bob replied, "Izzy, take some time off from your duties and take care of the daughter. I'll work on the funeral."

Helen and Gabby stayed with Izzy and were a big help consoling the young daughter.

The sniper attack failed to weaken the people Horseshoe for the planned frontal attack; however, one person was dead, and thirteen people were wounded including Jake, Bob, Maddie, and Will.

***

Jake was already in bed due to the pain pill that his dad gave him to help him sleep. His foot was going to be fine; however, the slow moving bullet struck the middle bone behind his middle toe, and it hurt like hell. The family was gathered at Bob's house on the deck in the dark. They didn't want to chance a sniper seeing them from across the river.

Bob poured everyone two fingers of Bourbon and made a toast, "To the best damn family and the most accurate snipers in the world. Those assholes won't mess with us again."

Jo added, "I have never been so scared in my life. Not for me but for each of you. I would give my life for any one of you."

"Everyone agreed and took a sip of the whiskey."

Jane spoke up and said, "I want our weddings to be this coming Wednesday. That hail of bullets made me worry about Bob, and I didn't want one of us to die before we get married."

"Momma Jane, I agree. Will and I want to be man and wife as soon as possible. I want to be Maddie Karr before the weekend."

"Jo said, "What will you two couples do about a honeymoon?"

Maddie quickly replied, "Will and I plan to go to Cancun or perhaps just stay in our trailer for a couple of days by ourselves. Missy, that means you need to move in the house."

"It's not like y'all haven't been acting like a married couple all along."

Will threw a sandal at her and said, "What have you and Matt been doing over at the abandoned barn. We saw you raking the straw out of your hair the other day."

"Will that's none of your business and Matt is my boyfriend."

Jo loudly said, "Time out kids. How old is Matt?"

"Mom, he's 18 and a great guy. I'm sorry I stirred the shit," Will replied.

"Will I'm not mad at you or Missy. It's just that this disaster has forced both of you to grow up quickly. I love you and know I can't keep you under my apron forever. Bill can you make a chastity belt?""

Missy was now four shades of red darker than she was when the shit hit the fan about Matt and said, "Mom, we've only kissed, and it's nobody's business.

Bill spoke up and said, "I wonder if any other family is having these kinds of conversations anywhere else in the world."

Jane replied, "I think we are all very opinionated, outspoken people and say what's on our minds. I sometimes worry that our poking into people's love lives might cause embarrassment to Will and Missy. I apologize up front but have to admit that we will probably keep doing it until they have kids of their own."

"I just don't want to hurt mom or dad during these discussions. I think the give and take of the teasing helps me through the day and I don't give a rat's ass what any of you think about what Maddie and I are doing between the sheets."

Jo raised her glass and said, "Spoken like a true Karr. Let's move the weddings to tonight."

Everyone laughed and then began drifting off to their rooms for the night.

Maddie and Will got in bed, and Will spooned up to Maddie's back to go to sleep. They lay there for a few minutes without saying anything as Will kissed her back around the wounds she suffered earlier in the day.

"Will, do you think it will ever be safe to have kids and raise a family?"

He kissed the nape of her neck and replied, "We need to keep being careful for about 3-6 months until the big die off is complete and then it will be as safe as it's going to get. I want to have our first child before all of the medical supplies run out. I also want us to go on a scavenging trip to find more antibiotics, so we'll have some when the kids are young. I wonder how long the pills and liquids last before going bad?"

"What do you want first? A boy or a girl?"

"I don't care as long as the baby is healthy and looks like you."

"Aw, that was sweet. We'll make warriors out of them boy or girl. I want my kids to be survivors."

"Amazon girls and Tarzan boys?"

She replied, "More like a Super Girl and Super Boy."

Maddie fell asleep in Will's arms thinking that her father had to be eradicated before she got pregnant. She didn't want that bastard around her kids.

*

Chapter 8

Day 13 - The Weddings

Maddie woke up when the alarm went off on the old wind-up clock. She lay in the bed with Will spooned against her back. He was trying to wake up as he yawned and wrapped his arms around her.

"You are going to be my wife today."

"And you are going to be my husband, and we can stop playing house and act like real married people do."

He pulled her close as his hands roamed over her body and said, "We can start now."

She pulled away, jumped out of bed, and replied, "We've started now a dozen times. I'm shocked your parents moved the kids out of our little camper. No, you have to behave and wait for our honeymoon. Surely you can wait 12 hours until after the reception."

"I might die of frustration before then."

"That's a chance I'm willing to take. I'm going over to make the coffee before mom wakes up. Get some clothes on and join me."

"Darn, Papaw warned me that they all change after they get a ring on their finger."

She jumped on top of him and began tickling him until he cried, "Stop."

"Say, uncle."

"Uncle."

Her warm body on top of him did nothing to ease his frustration as she pulled her shorts on and tied her halter. She walked out the door as he was dressing.

Bob, "I'm going to take a quick shower, and I think you should join me."

That ended up taking a bit longer than she planned and Maddie and Will were sipping on their first cup when they walked into the kitchen.

Jane hugged both and said, "My favorite couple. Let's fill up and go out on the deck. I love the early morning before the sun rises."

"Son, I want the family to all stay close to my house. I'd like to propose that we run down to Carthage and bring several of those modular houses back here for you and your dad. How does that sound?"

"Great. I agree on strength in numbers, and the privacy makes it work. By the way, you might want to lock the doors or at least close the bathroom door when you um...um...sing in the shower."

Jane popped him on the head and said, "Bob sings very well in the shower."

"TMI."

Maddie changed the conversation and said, "We're going to need everything from sheets to pots and pans."

"We got you covered from our many scavenging trips and Greg's hardware store. You won't need a thing."

Jo and Bill came dragging out of the house a half an hour later, and Jo's first words were, "That was some great singing in the shower this morning."

Her mom replied, "That's the pot calling the kettle black. It must have been. I see both of your hair is wet."

"That only underscores the need for Bill and me to get our own place. One of the campers will do, but we need something larger for the long haul. We still have Missy and Jake to consider before singing in the shower."

Maddie asked, "Will, has your family always said everything that enters their mind?"

"Yep, pretty much. When I was younger, I heard the adults talking and didn't know what I was hearing.

Now I'm just used to the crude jokes, teasing and sexual innuendo."

Bob replied, "I think he's talking about me."

"No, mom and dad are just as bad. Grandma Jane was always lady like until she started singing in the shower with you."

"So, I'm a bad influence?"

Maddie replied, "No, you are a sweet, joker who makes this family fun to be part of. I love every one of you, but Bob you are the spice that makes the family better."

Bob got up, walked over to Maddie and sat in her lap as he said, "This girl is a keeper. Will, you had better keep her happy."

Maddie pinched Bob's ass to get him to get off her lap and said, "My almost-husband keeps me very happy, and this family is icing on the cake."

Maddie and Jane took over Bob's house to get their hair done by Jo, makeup was done by Missy and dressed for the 1:00 wedding. The men were using Will's camper to get ready.

The wedding was at Greg's barn, and it had been decorated with streamers and hand painted signs to celebrate the occasion. One of the ordained deacons from the Baptist Church performed the ceremonies. Jane and Maddie were gorgeous in their wedding dresses.

Maddie's started out as a white evening gown that had been fitted to her slim body. Jane's dress was light blue and started life as a gown before removing the sleeves and adding a sash. Both of their veils had been made from a lace curtain. The men wore two of Bob's black suits with ties. Considering the world had fallen apart, they looked great as the weddings proceeded.

The reception was also held in the barn with plenty of food, beer, and wine. Bob was the life of the party as he cracked jokes and danced with Jane. Will danced with his new wife first, then his Mom and finally his Grandma Jane.

Jo had a smile as Will waltzed her around the dance floor and said, "Will I am so proud of the man you have become. You and Maddie were made for each other. She is beautiful and is a great fit for the family. I won't lie, son, I'm glad that you two are married now, and my first grandchild will be born in wedlock."

"Mom do you know something that I don't?"

"No, but as much as you two fooled around it wouldn't surprise me."

"Mom, trust me. She isn't pregnant."

"That's good but don't wait forever to have some grandkids."

"Will laughed and said. Wait, oh don't wait."

"She laughed and said, "You know what I mean."

"I do. I was just kidding."

The reception was going strong when Bob and Jane left in Bob's truck, and Will and Maddie left in one of the ATVs. Both had cans tied to the back and signs with Just Married on the back. Bob and Jane went to Bob's home, and Will drove to the camper. The people at the reception rotated out with the guards, so everyone was able to enjoy the event. The reception party was over just as the sun went down.

***

Several hours later Maddie and Will lay on the bed holding each other and looking at the rings on their hands hardly believing they were now man and wife.

Maddie looked out the window, saw the moon high in the sky, and said, "Are you game to go skinny dipping?"

"Hell yes!"

They gathered a blanket, their AR's, pistol belts and headed to the rocky bluff on the river.

Maddie saw Will grab the blanket and said, "We think alike."

They quietly walked past a noisy Max on their way to the river with Max following a few yards behind. The night was perfect with the half-moon in the sky and a gentle breeze. They quickly arrived at the bluff and shucked their clothes off. Will spread the blanket and they made love in the moonlight.

They were happy and carefree as they climbed down the rocks into the cool water and fooled around some more before going back up to the rocks to make love again. They were very occupied when they heard a vicious growl and a man scream. Will shined a flashlight and saw Max had a man's arm clamped in his teeth.

Maddie fired her AR three times as Will brought his rifle up to his shoulder. Will saw another man and cut him down with a well-placed shot. Several more shots were fired from the direction of the trailer. Maddie and Will were standing naked in the moonlight with their ARs, ready to fight.

"Y'all put some clothes on," called Grandma Jane.

Bob used his walkie-talkie to radio back that all was well and there were several bodies to dispose of over by the river bluff."

Maddie and Will scrambled to get dressed and then called for Bob and Jane to join them.

Bob walked up and said, "See Jane, I wasn't the only one who thought about skinny dipping in the moonlight on our wedding day."

"Jane replied, "Looks like Will and Maddie beat us to the river."

"Damn, those perverts were watching us from the bushes when Max attacked, or we would have been killed."

"I count five dead assholes. They were already over here, and it looks like they were going to raid our supplies judging from the empty bags piled beside them."

Jane asked, "Was the water cool?"

"Mom it was fantastic and y'all can have the river. Will and I have swum several times and will go back home now."

"Could y'all stay back in the bushes for a while and stand guard while we go for a swim?"

"We'd be glad as long as there isn't any hanky panky."

Bob replied, "I don't know about hanky, but there will be plenty of panky going on."

Jane must have pinched him because he cried out in pain as they scampered down the rocks to the water."

Maddie and Will found a place where they could be ready if needed and stayed on guard until Bob and Jane came back up to the top of the bluff.

Maddie told Will, "You know the world has changed when you have to stand guard while your grandparents are skinny dipping in the moonlight."

Will rubbed Max's ears and said, "We owe you a big steak."

"Son now you and Maddie need to keep some of the details to yourselves about our adventure tonight."

"Yes, that would be embarrassing for Jo to hear about what actually happened, Maddie replied."

It was 4:30 in the morning when they arrived back at Bob's house. Max jumped up on the deck and lay down beside the back door as they went into the house. Jane and Maddie stayed in the house while Bob grabbed several bottles of beer and took his grandson out under the stars.

Bob handed him a beer, and they sipped on the beer while waiting on the coffee.

Bob looked around and said, "How many men can say their wife shot a bunch of bad guys while standing naked in the moonlight?"

"I don't know Papaw, but it scared the shit out of me. Maddie reacted much faster and probably saved our asses."

"I hate for you two to start your marriage in this screwed up world."

"Papaw, the world was already pretty much screwed up before the lights went out. Now we just have to survive until the die off is complete and start a new better world."

"That's very astute of you to see it that way. Please remind me to keep a smile on my face."

"You always make everyone smile. I'll be glad to return the favor."

*

Chapter 9

Day 20 – Peace and Prosperity

The next two weeks were very peaceful, and the community was able to focus on making life better for all. Ben's team headed north to their new home and stayed in contact with Jim and Bob's communities. It was hard to imagine it was only three weeks since the lights went out since so much had changed in their world.

The steady stream of Walkers had dropped to a small but constant flow and the ones still on the road were filthy, diseased skeletons of the people they once were. It broke the community's heart that they couldn't help these people. The crops were just a few inches tall, and their supply of food would barely make it to the fall when the plants could be harvested.

The Walkers did bring them two schoolteachers, a doctor, and several mechanics that were vetted and allowed to join the community. Bob had the guards constantly looking for people who appeared to be clean, and disease free as the herd of people streamed by the Horseshoe, and they continued to find good people with usable skills. They also found some government officials who thought they should be in charge of the community and they were forcibly sent packing.

There hadn't been any more attacks since Maddie, and Will were caught with their pants down. The guards stayed vigilant, and they doubled the roving guards on horseback during the nights to stop any surprise attacks. Jim's community rooted out all of the near do wells and criminals across the river on the Horseshoe's east side, and Bob got volunteers to settle the land trapped in a loop of the river to the Horseshoe's west. He had the team actively looking for people to join that community that was also under his rule.

The land was shaped like an upside down teardrop with the narrow end only 550 yards wide. Bob sent an armed convoy with trucks towing bulldozers and a backhoe down through Carthage to the new land they now called the Little Horseshoe to construct a steel wall similar to the one at the Horseshow. The convoy was shot at a couple of times in the city of Carthage, but no one was wounded, and they killed two thugs.

The good news was that the owners had already planted their crops. The sad news was that the people attacking the Horseshoe killed them for their supplies and food without even thinking about growing crops. There were 18 empty homes in the Little Horseshoe that only needed the trash removed and a good cleaning to be homes for Bob's expanding community. Tony Fulkerson, Ned, and several other families moved over to occupy and farm the land.

Bob had sent several teams out to see if they could find any more pockets of good people banded together to survive among the outlaws and gangs. They brought back a mixed bag of information.

Many of the gangs had killed each other off in turf wars, but the ones that survived were getting stronger and had to find a steady source of food to survive. This meant small farming communities like theirs were the gang's primary target. There were also groups led by dictators like Senator O'Berg, who ruled with an iron fist but kept their people fed, so the folks tolerated the tyranny for the protection supplied.

There were three more groups that were refreshing islands of good hardworking people in this sea of filth, violence, and starvation. All had the same qualities that made them successful. All had a strong leader who guided his or her community of hardworking people who quickly plowed the ground and planted crops. Bob visited all three and took a few people from the community with him to exchange ideas on survival.

"Maddie, I want you and Will to join me on a trip to a small community called Pleasant Shade that is northeast of here and is about 12 miles away. Maddie, I want you to work with them to set up a barter and trade program. Remember we have doctors, mechanics, and teachers so we can trade skills as well as goods and rent construction equipment."

"I'd be honored to represent the community."

"Will, I need both of you to be on the lookout for any type of danger. Not just the obvious thugs. Look for anything that doesn't pass the smell test."

"Like people asking the wrong questions or people afraid to talk in front of their leaders?"

"You got my drift. Jane and Jo will spread out and talk with as many people as possible. I don't want to bring the fox into the hen house. Always keep your arms ready and stay alert. Danger can be around every corner."

They drove over in Bob's new old truck that Jo brought back in place of his that was stolen. He pulled a small trailer with a case of canned goods, several jars of honey, and a barrel full of freshly caught catfish to trade.

A few people tried to stop them on the way, but a wave of a rifle kept them at bay. The trip was uneventful, and they arrived in Pleasant Shade about 10:00 am. There were several clusters of houses, a closed general store, and a church within a small area. Bob drove up to a roadblock by a farmhouse where two men were working on a tractor, stopped, and got out unarmed with his palms up.

The guards said, "What the hell do you want and what's your name."

"I'm Bob Karr, and I need to talk to someone in charge."

"Follow me over to Ted's house. He's in charge of the guards."

Bob walked as Will followed in the truck over to the men.

"I'm Bob Karr, and I'm from south of here. We're out trying to see if any decent people have survived up this way."

The men were leery, but walked up to Bob and introduced themselves.

Bob asked, "Do y'all have any trouble makers around? I see you both have pistols strapped to your hips."

"And your people have ARs ready to tear us up if we reach for them."

"That's right. We are very careful around strangers, and you should be too. .We are looking for good communities to trade with and perhaps help each other out in a pinch. We have four small communities in this area that are slowly running the criminals away and want to know if y'all might be a fit for our group. Do you have a leader?"

"Well, not an elected one, but Alice Jones pretty much runs things. She and her husband were doomsday preppers long before the shit hit the fan and helped us survive this mess. We've had our troubles and had to use these guns more than we like. I'll take you to her if my son and I can get a ride."

Will followed the man's direction down a side street to a dirt road and they went to the end where there was a two-story log home.

This is Alice and Fred's place.

The front door opened and a woman came walking out with an AR pointing at them, and a man came up from behind them with an AR.

"Drop your guns, or we shoot."

"Lady, I'm Bob Karr, and we're not dropping our weapons. You might get a couple of us, but we have four guns to your two. We don't want to shoot, but we have killed many thugs and gang members and have gotten good at it so why don't we both drop our muzzles and start talking about how we can help each other."

The man in the back of the truck said, "Alice, lower your rifle. I don't want to find out who is the best shot sitting in the middle of your targets."

Alice and her husband lowered their guns at the same time Bob's people lowered theirs.

"As I said, I'm Bob Karr, and we drove over here to see if we can trade with you and perhaps see how we can help each other out. We have doctors, nurses, teachers, bulldozers, and plenty of fish."

"Where are you from?"

"South of Dixon Springs."

"Y'all are the ones who cleaned out several biker gangs and massacred hundreds of those walking assholes who keep trying to steal our food. The flow dried up over this way once the word got out that y'all shoot thieves."

"I guess that's us. We brought some things to trade with you."

Jane and Jo mingled with the locals while Bob and Maddie haggled with the leaders about trading. After several lengthy discussions, Bob learned that about the only things they had to trade were gasoline, fish, and goat meat. They had about 50 head of cattle to build up the herd for the future. Bob could see hundreds of goats wandering around in a fenced in an enclosure behind her house.

"Would you trade some goats for what we have in the back of the truck? I'd like to start breeding goats at our place. We only have about ten cows and a bunch of chickens."

"We'll give you two breeding pairs for what's in your truck, and we need to trade you for some medical help."

"Sounds fair to me on the goats. What kind of medical help do you need?"

"One of our kids busted his arm, and we have a woman with a bad tooth."

"Bring them down to Dixon Springs. Head south on Rome Road, go about a half mile and ask for Bill Karr at our gate. Bill will treat them free this time and then from then on he will charge a reasonable fee. He needs all of the medical supplies that you can scrounge up, so he will always trade services for medical supplies."

They exchanged items and loaded the goats into the back of the pickup. They were about to drive away when they heard, "Maddie. Maddie is that you?"

"Ms. Gregory? Where have you been?"

The woman ran to Maddie, and they hugged for a minute and cried before they began to talk.

"Maddie I thought you were dead or carried off by those hooligans. They attacked in the middle of the night the lights went out."

"No, I went out of my mind when I saw my mom dead in the bus. I took what money she had and bought some supplies at a sporting goods store and got out of there. I knew the shit would hit the fan when the jocks started drinking. I didn't want to stay around and find out what they'd do to me."

Ms. Gregory heard what Maddie said, hung her head down and cried as she mumbled, "The bastards raped me. Seventeen-year-old boys that were in my classroom ripped my clothes off and raped me. I wanted to kill them that night. They finally got tired of me and raped several of the students before heading south to Nashville.

That's one of the reasons I left in a hurry. Young men drinking at the end of the world can't bring good things."

"What are you doing now?"

"I'm trying to work my way back to Nashville."

"Ms. Gregory, Nashville is a war zone of gangs, drugs, and violence. Why don't you come and stay with us? We have a small community that is safe, and we are growing crops. You'd have to work like the rest of us, but you'd be safe."

Maddie waved at the others to come and meet Ms. Gregory.

Joan Gregory was 38, had auburn hair, and was five foot six inches tall. She was very attractive and very outgoing. She had been divorced for several years and lived alone with her dog.

Ms. Gregory this is my husband, Will Karr, his mom Jo Karr, his grandmother Jane and his grandfather Bob Karr. This is my teacher and friend Joan Gregory.

"Your husband?"

"Yes. Things have moved at the speed of sound since the lights went out. I'll give you the long story later. You can stay with Will and me until we find you a long-term home."

They all shook hands, and Bob welcomed her to join them at the Horseshoe.

"I don't want to put you out."

"You won't because you will earn your keep. We all work together, pull guard duty together and have fun together. We need another good teacher. What did you teach?"

"Biology and agriculture."

"That's fantastic. We will definitely need your knowledge to sustain our farming efforts."

Jane caught Jo's eye and said, "We need to find a single man for her."

Jo replied, "With a body like that, it had better be real soon. The men will be drooling."

The trip back to the Horseshoe was uneventful, and Maddie and Joan sat up front with Will so they could get caught up on events during the time since the lights went out. Joan had slowly wandered south, avoiding people as much as possible. She walked into Pleasant Shade hungry and barely alive. She was lucky one of the farm families found her and took her in before their leader could stop them.

Maddie introduced Joan to the family and promised to introduce her to the others at the first meeting.

***

The meeting was over, and Joan walked up to Greg and said, "Greg Farmer, don't I know you?"

"Mam, I believe I would remember you," he replied and walked away.

*

Chapter 10

Day 20 – Rebellion in Wilson County

The Senator gave a pep talk to his followers in the school gym about 10:00 that night. He told them, "Men and women of Lebanon. You have God and country on your side because your cause is just. The rebels have captured the farms north, south and west of our fair city. They won't stop until they have all of the farmland around our city and starve us to death. This tyranny must end!"

Walt and his deputies led the cheering, and soon the crowd was whipped into a frenzy. The Senator looked around the room and saw sixty-three loyal warriors who would be going out that night to conquer the enemy and enable them to obtain food for their people.

They loaded into the waiting trucks and left to attack their targets. There were ten trucks with six-man teams who would attack the homes of the resistance leaders. Walt would lead the attack on Jim Dickerson's house and had three extra men on his team to assure success. The attacks were scheduled for 1:00 am to catch the families sleeping. Each group had been instructed to kill every living being found at the house.

Jim and Hoss were out in the barn tending to a sick calf when Hoss saw the lights heading their way. The trucks were a mile away, and Jim knew they would soon be under attack. They grabbed their guns, woke up their wives and Hoss's kids, and sent them down to the river in an ATV without the lights on. Jim radioed Bob and asked Bob to send a team over to protect his family until they could get across the river. Jim and Hoss would lie in wait for the attackers to stall them long enough for their family to reach safety. Jim had a couple of tricks up his sleeves for the SOBs.

Jim attached the wires to the fuses for the dynamite bombs at the preset positions and backed off to their hiding spot while the bastards snuck up to their house. Everyone had placed covers over their pillows so the intruders would think they caught the family asleep. When the bastards were all in the house, Jim would spring the first trap.

Hoss pointed to the black shape sneaking up the back steps about the same time Jim saw the flashlight come on in the family room. All of the bedrooms were upstairs, so Jim gave them a minute and got ready to push the first switch. Gunshots and flashes were coming from the house when Jim flipped the switch that set off ten sticks of dynamite in the place. A massive explosion threw pieces of the house hundreds of feet into the air, and then a giant ball of flames as the house caught on fire.

Jim then saw a pickup turn its lights on and surge toward the burning house. He waited until it was close to one of the preset bombs and flipped the second switch. The truck flipped end over end as it exploded when the gas tank ruptured. Two men covered in flames ran across the lawn and dropped as they died. Another truck turned its lights on, but this truck headed back to town at full speed.

Jim and Hoss jumped into an ATV and headed to the river where they were met by Bob and six on his team including Jane and Will.

"Bob the bastards tried to kill us in our sleep; I guess they had several hit squads out tonight. Can I use your radio to contact my team?"

Bob handed him a walkie-talkie and said, "Come on over to our home for the night. We'll get a plan to take out that damn Senator in the morning."

Only one of Jim's men answered, and his farm was under attack, so the call was short.

"Bob, if you'll loan me an ATV or a pickup, Hoss, and I will round up all of our group and start an attack on Lebanon tonight. Those bastards won't stop at killing the leaders."

"Wait a minute. Don't you think that the Senator and Walt will think you and your family were killed in the explosion? That will give you time to plan an attack instead of reacting."

"Well, I guess you are right. Let's go to your place."

They didn't see or hear Walt's spy in the bushes by the river. Nor did Bob ever expect one of his most loyal people to be a spy for the Senator.

***

Senator, we eliminated all but one of the leaders and their family. Dickerson's place exploded during the attack. Our entire team died with him and his family; however, the important thing is that we killed everyone in the house.

Walt, this calls for a toast to the success of our community and the annexation of the eastern section over to the river.

The door burst open, and a man walked in and said, "Dickerson and his family are safely at Karr's place. Their guards heard you coming, and they left for the river while Hoss and Jim stayed to set off explosive charges to kill the hit squad. They are regrouping tomorrow and coming after you two with a large army."

"Thanks. Do they suspect you?"

"No, the idiots have me on several committees aimed at killing you and making their community safe.

"We will send a squad over to kill all of the Karr and Dickerson families. Walt, get your team's ass in gear and attack them before dawn. You get back over there and divert the guards from this side of the Horseshoe or kill them. Stay away from Karr's house.

It was now 2:30 and Walt scrambled to get his team plus several boats over to the river. The boats were waiting; they loaded their gear into the vessels and began rowing to the other side.

"I need you to move over to the wall. We just received word that an attack is planned against us tonight."

"I can't leave this section unguarded, "Izzy said as he saw his friend shoot him in the gut with the silenced pistol.

Izzy lay bleeding and said, "Why?"

"Because the Senator has plans for the Horseshoe."

Izzy died knowing that one of his friends was a traitor."

The path was now open for the hit squad to attack the Karr house.

***

"Maddie, wake up," Will said as he gently shook her shoulder.

Her eyes opened, and Will planted a kiss on her lips, and then said, "Let's go skinny dipping down at the rock bluff."

"I'm in. Let's go and get wet. Grab your gear."

They were barely dressed when Will heard Max growl and a man scream. Will and Maddie looked outside and saw men swarming around the back of the house. Will turned his flashlight on and shined the light on them. They turned and started shooting at the trailer.

Maddie and Will returned fire on the men, and they scrambled for cover as Will and Maddie both shot and killed one each. Several were already in the house, and there were flashes of light along with the sound of intense gunfire in every room of the house.

Bob and Jane had been on the back deck a few minutes before the attackers arrived and heard them approach the house. Bob woke the others up and told them to prepare for an attack.

Joan came running from her room, and Maddie knocked her down to the floor as bullets ripped through the trailer. Maddie shot one attacker in the head ending his sorry life. Will wounded two more, and the fight was over at the back of the house. They ran into the kitchen and shot two men in the back before the men knew someone was behind them. Suddenly the shooting was over. There was silence for a minute, followed by screams and crying. Jo was holding Jake's lifeless body on the floor, and Jim Dickerson's wife was crying as she and her daughter in law held on to Hoss' bullet-riddled body. One of Jim's granddaughters was also killed in the battle.

There were seven dead men in the house, and six outside that had attempted to kill both families.

Will had been shot on the left side of his chest, but the bullet just scrapped a rib leaving a furrow on Will's side. Bob's left hand was hit by a ricocheted, and Bill caught a round in his right forearm. None of the wounds was severe, and Jane and Bill tended to the wounded.

The Karr and Dickerson families grieved while Jack added guards around the house and sent several down to the river to see why the guard hadn't warned them.

Jo and Jane spent the morning getting Jake's body ready for burial while Will dug a grave behind Bob's house out by a big oak tree. Both families were in shock and wondered how O'Berg and Walt had become so evil.

***

Jim those bastards knew the layout of my house and which room I slept in. They also knew which room you were in. They hit those rooms first from the outside. If I hadn't heard them approaching and Will and Maddie hadn't killed several of them we'd all be dead," said Bob.

"I couldn't sleep so I talked Maddie into going for a moonlit swim when we heard the men outside."

Jack drove up with Greg, and they had Izzy's body in the bed.

"Bob, one of the bastards shot Izzy in the stomach and let him bleed out. That's why we didn't get any warning from the guard on the river."

Joan took Maddie off to the side and asked, "Do you really believe that your dad is behind this attack?"

"Yes. He has become a power-mad dictator over in Lebanon. He had his sheriff shoot women and kids the other day as they tried to steal food from a store. He made several of the cities prominent leaders disappear."

Joan replied, "Then you need to know that Greg Farmer and your dad are close friends. Greg is very wealthy and is the money behind the Senator's run for the presidency. I worked for the Senator right out of college while I worked on my master's degree. Your dad got too friendly, and I left."

"Oh shit. He is a trusted member of our community. I'll get Bob off to the side and let him know. Please keep this to yourself."

"I will. Be careful."

Joan continued to give Maddie more detail about Greg's role and friendship with the Senator.

Maddie caught Will off to the side and said, "Joan just told me that Greg Farmer has been a major donor and supporter of the Senator's for a long time."

"Oh shit. He is a spy in our ranks. Is Joan sure?"

"Yes, she worked for dad right out of college and saw Greg at dad's office many times. Greg and the

Senator went on expensive vacations, and Greg supplied the women who went with them."

"Maddie, I'm sorry that you had to hear such sordid details about your father."

"It just confirmed what I already knew about the piece of shit. I disowned him long ago and would shoot him on sight if he ever came around here. Let's go catch Papaw Bob."

"Well shit. I suspected there was a spy in our group, but I never suspected that Greg could spy on us much less kill Izzy, "Bob exclaimed after hearing what Maddie had to say.

"I'm sorry about Greg. I know he was a good friend of yours."

"The son of a bitch will pay for what he did. I have to calm down and figure out how to use Greg to set the Senator up for an ass whooping. I'm only going to bring Jo, Jack, Jane and you two into the fold on this one. We need to meet after the funeral and set a trap that will end the Senator's rule of Lebanon and kill him and that scumbag, Walt Long.

The funeral for Jake was held that morning in Bob's backyard, and they laid him to rest in the grave that Will dug under the oak tree. Everyone was in tears as they placed the young lad in his grave, but Jo was torn to pieces seeing her innocent boy stricken down before he had a chance to grow into manhood. Helen also saw her new boyfriend struck down before she got a chance to know him.

They left Jo by the grave with Bill and went to the center of the Horseshoe to the community graveyard to bury Izzy and Jim Dickerson's family members. The service was short, and only the immediate family stayed after the service to mourn the dead. The rest had to get on with the full-time job of survival.

"Papaw, we need to get the SOBs massed together thinking that they are about to trap us when we spring our trap on them," Will said.

Jane replied, "How will we know that Greg has tipped off the Senator?

Bob replied, "Because Jack and Will will shadow Greg after we cover the fake plans with the team. Since the time of the meeting, until we attack will only be about three hours, Greg will have to haul ass over to the Senator or use a walkie-talkie to contact the Senator. When we know the Senator has been contacted, bring Greg to me."

Jack replied, "I know how that song ends."

"Damn Skippy. I'll put a bullet in his gut like he did to Izzy and watch the bastard die."

The discussion went on for an hour, and they had a plan to end the dictatorship of Lebanon. Bob called a meeting for the regular leadership and told them about his and Jack's plan. There were several questions; however, the leaders were pleased with the plan and wanted payback for the people lost or wounded by the SOBs.

Greg excused himself by saying, "I'll meet y'all at the staging area. I have to check on Betty Lou before we leave."

Greg headed straight to his barn closely followed by Jack and Will. He entered the barn and took a radio from a box hidden under some hay.

He turned the radio on and said, "This is Charlie. This is Charlie."

"Go, Charlie. This is Lucy."

"Charlie, you are going to be attacked ..."

Will heard the bastard give the details for the plan for the attack that night. Will waved at Jack after Greg stored the radio and they followed Greg back to Bob's house.

Jack caught Bob and told him that the rat had passed on the information and the trap just had to be set.

Jim had been sent to meet with his forces and was told where to stage his men and what his assignment was.

Bob stood in front of his troops and said, "We are heading to a staging area south of Lebanon after dark and then at 3:00 am, we will stage in an abandoned grocery store about 600 yards south of the police station and city hall. Jim's team will join us there. At 3:30 am, we will move out to our targets. We will send groups of five-man teams out to specific objectives to eliminate. I will lead a thirty-man squad with the mission to kill the Senator and his staff. Jim will have two similar teams and destroy the police force.

The success of this mission is predicated on total surprise. We have to infiltrate the area without being seen and then get to our targets without being detected. By daylight, all of the bad guys will be dead."

Also, the above is precisely what Greg told Walt Long. Walt told the Senator, and then Walt filled his key men in on the plot. He planned to have his men in the staging building and the buildings around that building so he could kill all of the rebels in one surprise attack. He would concentrate his forces for maximum efficiency.

Bob called the leaders together in a surprise meeting and said, "Men it's time to head to the south of Lebanon.

Greg said, "Did our plans change? It's just a little after 2:00."

"Yes, those plans have been scrapped, and we are now sending the teams directly to their targets."

Greg's face turned red, and he started to leave when Jack took his weapon and pushed him back into the meeting at gunpoint.

"Team, this rat has been passing information on to the Senator and personally killed Izzy. He is responsible for the deaths of our family and team members. Greg why?"

Greg lunged for Jack's pistol, and Jack shot him in the chest during the struggle. The shot tore his heart apart, and he died quickly. Most of the team was stunned and tried to make sense of what had just played out in front of them.

Bob spoke up and filled the silence, "Greg Farmer has been working with the Senator all along. He has helped coordinate the attacks by the Walkers and several biker gangs. It wasn't a coincidence that we were always attacked when we were the most vulnerable. Men load up. We have things to do and people to kill."

Will asked, "Papaw, what is the special assignment that you gave Grandma and Maddie?"

"What? Maddie told me to check with you and that she had something to do. Will they're grown assed women and I know Jane and Maddie can take care of themselves. We have people to kill, and my guess is, so do they.

Maddie and Jane were in Jane's Volkswagen heading to Lebanon.

*

Chapter 11

Day 20 – The Wraiths and Rat Killing Time.

"Maddie it's time for you to join me on my next outing as the Wraith. You know the Senator won't even be close to the fighting or be caught in the trap. Are you up to helping me kill the Senator, Walt Long, and anyone else around them when we find the sorry bastards?"

"Yes, I am. They are vermin who need to be exterminated. Jane, I was always a strong willed person. I have grown into a strong woman who can do what it takes to survive. I want to help you get rid of the criminals, thugs, and filth that hang around in the shadows and escape punishment."

"I knew that would be your answer. What does Will think about this?"

"Will is okay with the elimination of the trash; he just doesn't want me to get hurt. He wants to go on the missions with me and help guard me against danger."

"That's a good idea in general, but won't work this time. We are going to sneak into the Senator's camp in broad daylight pretending to be women who want to take care of the Senator's sexual needs. The bastard has a small harem and adds to them anytime he finds women who pass his inspection. This work will up close and personal with knives. Do you think your dad will recognize you?"

"No, he's only seen me twice in the last two years, and I've matured a bit. I don't like killing, but I'll like this work."

"We need to be ready to head to Lebanon this evening. Get your shortest shorts and a halter top. We need to show our goods to catch the Senator's eye. Place your .380 in your waistband holster, and it probably will be confiscated. If not we have a couple of pistols."

They drove over to Hartsville and down to Lebanon and then stopped at a roadblock at Highway 141 as it entered the city limits. They were told to get out of the car and were searched for weapons and contraband. The guards found both .380s and handcuffed the women for bringing guns into the city. Both guards made lewd jokes about personally punishing them for breaking the law.

Jane said, "We were going to Lebanon to see the Senator. We heard he likes gorgeous women and treats them well. It's not good for single women out there these days."

"Well we get a few of you each day, and the Senator's harem is all full. You lucky women get to be Phil and my women. We will treat you right if you do what you are told to do."

Jane demanded to see the Senator and was pushed into the back seat of a car and told to strip down.

Maddie pulled her driver's license from her back pocket and said, "That's me, and I'm the Senator's daughter. Look."

The guard looked at Maddie and the license and asked, "Why were you trying to sneak in acting like whores?"

"We wanted to surprise my dad. My mom is his ex-wife, and we wanted to surprise him."

"Oh shit. Mam, I was just kidding. Please get out of the car, and we'll get you a ride to the Senator's office."

"Phil, radio the Senator's office and tell him his daughter and ex-wife are being transported to his office."

The man called the Senator's aide, and the aide told him the Senator was tied up in a meeting, but they should bring the ladies on in to see the Senator. A car arrived a few minutes later, and Maddie and Jane were taken to see the Senator. They had lost their guns but still had their ceramic knives taped to the small of their backs under their blouses.

They arrived at City Hall, and both were escorted into the Senator's private area and offered drinks and sandwiches. A woman came into the room and said, "Maddie, I recognize you from the pictures on the Senator's desk. Who is the woman with you? I met your mother years ago, and this is not her."

Maddie quickly answered, "Mam, I'm sorry for the deception; however, this woman has saved my life on several occasions and is just like a mother to me."

Jane spoke, "I'm Joan Gregory, and I was one of Maddie's teachers at her high school. We were on a field trip when the lights went out. We've been on our own and ever since surviving the best we could."

They finished their sandwiches while Jane surveyed the room looking for anything that could be used as a weapon. Both women left them alone in the room, and Jane signaled that the room might be bugged, so they kept the conversation to topics that helped solidify their story.

The first woman came back into the room to bring more drinks and to take away the empty plates.

"Mam, where is the restroom?"

"Oh, just go through that door and make a left. It's the third door on the right. Just don't try to go out the exit door. The guard will send you back to me."

They went into the restroom and checked it for potential weapons, cameras, and bugs. They found nothing usable, finished their business, and walked back to the room they were held in, while waiting for the

Senator. All of the doors were locked along the hallway. They were given several magazines and a couple of crossword puzzles to pass the time since the lady told them that the Senator was in a very long meeting.

Jane whispered to Maddie, "I'll bet the meeting includes a couple of young blondes."

The Senator was in fact in the company of a red head and a blonde for the rest of the afternoon. His staff knew not to disturb the Senator when he was in his special meetings. This meeting went into overtime, and the Senator wasn't finished until 6:00 pm, and then he took one of the women to dinner before coming back to the office. He had been told while he was cleaning up that his daughter was waiting on him at the office.

"Make her comfortable, and I'll be back when I get back."

The two women who were attending to Jane and Maddie were now pissed that they had to stay over and babysit the Senators brat of a daughter. They were getting a bit short with Maddie when a young blonde woman came into the room.

"Maddie, my dear. I'm your stepmother. I married your dad after your mom left him. You are so beautiful. I want you to come to our house and dine with me."

"Hello, I'd love to. Can my dear friend come with us?"

She paused for a second and replied, "Of course. A friend of yours is a friend of mine and your father."

An older limousine took them to the Senator's home, and several maids and a butler took care of them. They were each given a room, and formal eveningwear was laid out on their beds. When they came downstairs, they were given cocktails and conversed with the Senator's wife until a maid came in and told them that dinner was ready.

A rather attractive young man seated them and served them during the meal. Maddie saw him stroke her stepmother's inner thigh when they thought no one could see.

"Maddie said, "I like your butler. I need one of them for myself."

"He comes in handy and a big help when the Senator is in those long meetings."

Maddie replied, "I'll bet he services you very well. Is he good in bed?"

Her stepmother laughed and said, "Actually he is great in bed. You see the Senator has his flings and I have mine. It's hard to find a good man these days, and Jose is a good man when I need him. If your mom had been more open minded, she would still have the Senator."

Maddie stifled her typical smart assed remark and said, "Mom was never good at sharing her men. I, on the other hand, don't mind sharing."

"Well, if you won't tell your father, I'll send Jose up to your room tonight. He will make you feel like a special woman."

Jane interrupted, "Damn, you young chicks are talking all around me. I have needs also."

"Jose can stop by your room after he has pleased Maddie. I share my toys."

It was half past 8:00 when the Senator came strolling into the room, gave his wife a peck on the cheek, and picked Maddie up and hugged her.

"My dear Maddie, tell me all about your last few weeks. I hope they weren't too bad. I hear this charming young lady saved your life," the Senator said as he kissed Jane's hand.

Maddie looked at Jane and saw a very attractive woman who could pass for 35, and she saw that the Senator couldn't take her eyes off Jane or her well-shaped body. He was smitten by her, and she played him with every trick she knew. She laughed at his jokes, wiggled what needed to be wiggled, and ran her fingers on his thigh when no one could see.

They retired for drinks in the study, and the maid served brandy while Maddie filled them in on their travels. She kept most of it as accurate as possible so their stories would match if needed. Soon it was time to retire, and they went to their own rooms. The Senator told Jose to keep his wife busy while attending to his guests. He took a bottle of wine and two glasses to Jane's room and knocked.

Jane ushered him into the room and said, "I was wondering how long it would take you to get to my room. I'll cut the crap and tell you that ever since Maddie told me about you on the trip, I've had a crush on you. She wasn't wild about coming here, but I convinced her to come so I could meet you."

"Well, I'm so glad she did. You are stunning in the gown."

Jane dropped the gown to the floor and was now standing before him in a bra and panties as she said, "Pour me a glass of that wine and let's get to know each other."

He tried getting his hands on her, and she stroked his ego by asking him to tell her about himself. That was probably the only thing that could get his mind off having sex with Jane. Their plan was that Jane would keep him occupied while Maddie knocked out a guard and took his weapons.

Maddie snuck out of her room wearing her shorts and blouse as she avoided being seen by the staff. There were three guards roving around the outside and only one on the inside. Finally one of the outside guards came into use the bathroom and Maddie walked into the bathroom behind him. When he finished and came out of the stall Maddie, hit him on the back of the head with a heavy vase and killed the poor lad. She took his clothes, battle gear, and weapons and dressed quickly in his clothes. She stuck his body in the stall and locked the door.

Maddie was sneaking back toward Jane's room when Jose came out of a room and walked into her. He was confused at first and then knew something was wrong. Maddie grabbed him with one hand on his side and shoved a knife deep into his chest. He muttered a few words as he died in her arms.

Maddie slowly opened the door to Jane's room and saw the Senator sitting in a chair with Jane on the bed. Maddie waved the knife and Jane reached up and dropped her bra to the floor. The Senator stood up and buried his face in Jane's chest as Maddie drove the knife into his back where she thought his heart was located.

He turned and said, "Maddie, why?"

"Because you are a piece of shit and left me like an unwanted puppy. Die bastard," Maddie said as she stabbed him a dozen more times."

"That's enough girl. It looks like a slaughterhouse in here. We have to get the hell out of here before anyone comes looking for the Senator."

Jane put her shorts and blouse on, and then took the rifle leaving Maddie a 9mm pistol and the knife. They peeked out the door, and no one was up in the house, so they calmly walked down the stairs and slipped out the back door. They were half way across the back yard when all hell broke loose as lights came on and someone shot at them.

"Maddie, it's Walt long and his deputies. Kill all of the bastards."

They dropped behind a stone wall but were outnumbered and had to make a run for it before they were flanked. Jane told Maddie to run, and she would cover her retreat. Jane shot as fast as she could and knocked two men down. Maddie was now in place. She gave covering fire for Jane as she ran across the lawn. She joined Maddie, and they ran as fast as possible when a bullet struck Jane in the back and knocked her down. Maddie fired back at the shooter, got Jane to her feet, quickly got into the shadows, and then helped Jane away from the house and down a back alley. She talked to Jane and kept her moving until she pushed her into a yard barn at the back of a house a few blocks from the Senator's home.

Jane had lost a lot of blood and was barely breathing when Maddie tore off part of her blouse and used it to apply pressure to her wound. Then Maddie realized a larger exit wound was under Jane's right breast. She was bleeding to death, and Maddie was powerless to stop her death.

Maddie held Jane as she died and knew that she had lost her mother again. God had given Jane to her to replace her mother, and now some asshole had taken her away. Maddie laid Jane down on the floor, kissed her, and went back to the Senator's home to complete some unfinished business.

Maddie worked her way back to the house in the shadows and arrived as Walt Long, and a deputy got in their truck and left. Maddie ran through several homes and beat them to the corner. Maddie saw Walt on the passenger side take a drink from a steel flask and pass it to the driver. She took aim at the driver's head, pulled the trigger, and the bullet struck the driver above the left ear, causing his head to explode. The inside of the truck was covered in the driver's blood and bits of skull and brain.

Maddie saw Walt reach for his gun but was faster as she again aimed, pulled the trigger, and shot Walt Long in the chest.

She ran to the vehicle, knocked the pistol from Walt's hand, and said, "Jo Karr told me to send you to hell if I ever met you. Well GO TO HELL," she said as she shot him in the heart and the head.

Maddie took all of their weapons, threw the bodies out on the curb, and drove away in the Sheriff's truck. She stopped by an abandoned clothing store, found some black clothes that fit her and became the Wraith that night. She went on to the town hall, captured the guard, and forced him to tell her which of the town's leaders and politicians threw in with her father. After she had found what she wanted, she killed the guard and went house to house killing eight more of the people who had made Lebanon a dictatorship.

Maddie killed the last one and then painted a note on the front door of City Hall stating, *"I killed the Senator, Walt Long, six of his deputies and the eight assholes who betrayed you and helped Senator O'Berg screw this city. - The Wraith.*

Maddie stayed in the shadows as she watched the police search for the people who killed the senator. Suddenly the cops were called to another situation. Maddie guessed that Bob had created that situation. She walked up behind the guard at the back of the house, slit his throat, took his rifle and pistol, and moved to the front of the house. She dispatched this guard with the same efficiency, and then walked into the house, killed the butler who tried to shoot her, and then sent all of the staff away.

She climbed the stairs, found her stepmother's room, and found her dead on the floor with an empty bottle of sleeping pills on her nightstand.

Maddie said to herself, "Well, my job is done here. I'm going back to keep Jane company until Bob and Will finish off all of the assholes, bastards, and perverts."

Maddie quickly fell asleep beside Jane and didn't wake up until Will woke her after the sun came up.

***

Bill stayed back with Jo as they began the grieving process for their son Jake who had been struck down so young. Will drove over to the staging area below Lebanon with his Papaw and six other of the team. Thirty-three men and women from the Horseshoe and 55 from Jim Dickerson's group gathered in three different locations around the town. Bob and half of his team were in a woods just west of the Senator's home, while Jack had the other half headed toward the key members of the Senator's loyal staff.

Jim's two teams were tasked with killing all of the police force and anyone else who showed up at the grocery store where they expected to trap Jim's team. Jim saw the deputies and several of the town's near do wells surrounding the grocery store. He held his men back until they were all in place.

Bob's teams were infiltrating the exclusive gated community that the Senator resided in when they heard gunfire from the Senator's home. They continued to the house carefully and got into a gunfight with several of the Senator's bodyguards. They quickly dispatched the bodyguards and entered the Senator's home to find someone had stabbed the Senator multiple times and he was lying in a pool of his own blood. They searched the area around the house and found several more bodyguards that had been stabbed or shot. None was alive.

"Damn, someone got to the bastard first. Who the hell could have done this without us knowing? Let's move out and hook up with Jack's team."

They walked down the long drive and found the bodies of Walt Long and a deputy dead on the sidewalk.

"Holy shit! Someone beat us to Walt. These guys made some serious enemies."

Will replied, "Looks like the Wraiths have been busy tonight."

"Son, you don't think that Jane and Maddie killed all of these men. Do you?"

"I do. The Senator was stabbed a dozen times, and usually, that means someone hated the scumbag. Maddie really hated him. Besides the killing looks like what Grandma was doing to the gangs east of the horseshoe."

"Well, whoever did the dirty deeds saved us a lot of work? Let's go help, Jack. I'll get him on the radio."

Bob keyed the mic and said, "Our job's done. We're coming to assist you."

"Come on over to City Hall. Someone killed every son of a bitch that threw in with Long and the Senator."

Bob replied, "Damn, that's what we found at the Senator's place."

"Did the Wraiths leave a message?"

"No, we'll be there in five minutes.

Bob surveyed the damage at City Hall, and Jack filled him in on the dead supporters of the Senator to his amazement.

Jack said, "I believe the Wraith took out all of my targets and killed the last one a few minutes before we arrived at the first house. None of the spouses or children were killed. Several wives watched their husbands get shot by a person dressed in black with black women's hose stretched over their face. I asked if the attacker was a man or women and they didn't know. The best they could do is to tell me the person was about 5 foot seven and had athletic builds."

"Screw it, Jack! I don't care who they were. I'm just glad they are on our side," Bob added

Jim's teams had the police station and the grocery store covered and attacked as soon as the police charged into the grocery store.

There were 15 deputies and 12 men who were deputized for the attack on the store. They threw flash bangs and hand grenades into the store before breaking down the doors and entering the building. It was apparent to Jim the police did not intend to take anyone alive.

Jim's first team shot all of the men and women left outside and then stood guard while team two enter the building from the front door and the loading dock at the rear of the building. The police were outnumbered and outgunned but refused to surrender.

Jim yelled, "Throw your guns down, raise your hands and slowly exit the building, and you will live. You have 10 seconds to surrender before we kill every one of you."

A fusillade of gunshots toward Jim's position was their answer. Jim and his men returned fire while making sure they kept behind cover. Jim didn't want to lose any men to get rid of these criminals, so he asked two of his team to make some Molotov cocktails. This took about five minutes, and he told them to chuck several into both entrances to the store. The store was engulfed in flames when the so-called police tried to escape. Jim and his men picked them off as they tried to escape.

One of the women on the team was upset that they killed the men as they tried to save themselves from the flames.

"Brenda, those men were offered safety and turned it down. They would have killed all of us and never given us a chance to surrender. Suck it up buttercup."

The attack on the police station was over as soon as it started. There were only two men and a woman on duty, and all three were taken out by snipers. They never knew what hit them. Jim walked over to the police station and thanked the men and women who captured the police station.

"I can't thank you enough for helping us free this town from the scum. You put your lives on the line to stop the assholes from killing us, and you liberated the town. Now we need to manage the city until elections can be held to install honest God fearing people into the key positions."

Jim caught several of the citizens that were good friends and asked them to spread the word in the morning that he would address the town at the high school gym and fill them in on the events that night. His friends couldn't believe the Senator and the Sheriff had been killed and were ready to celebrate.

He told them, "We still have some work to do to prevent some other asshole from trying to take over the town. Be ready for a few more small fights. Tell everyone to meet at the high school at 7:00 pm. We need some breakfast and a good day's sleep."

***

Papaw, I radioed dad, and he told me that Grandma and Maddie haven't been seen since yesterday evening."

"Son we need to search for them now. One might have been wounded."

Bob thought might have been injured or worse but didn't say it aloud.

"Jack, I'm taking Will and a couple of men to search the area around the Senator's mansion for Maddie and Jane. Could you search the homes of the Senator's people and also send a vehicle to check the road back to the Horseshoe."

"Oh shit. I never put two and two together. We'll get right on it boss."

Will and Bob drove back to the Senator's home, parked on the street where the bodies had been found and started to walk towards the mansion when Will exclaimed, "See that VW. Let's check it out."

They walked over to a car that someone pulled off the street behind some bushes and Will opened the doors.

"Papaw, that's Maddie's backpack. Is the other one Grandma's?"

"Damn, it is hers. Well we know they were here, and my guess is that they are still here or they would have driven the Bug back home. Will, let's do a room-by-room search of the house. You two search the grounds. If we don't find them, we'll start searching the neighborhood."

Will and Bob went room to room being careful that there might still be hostiles in the area. They searched the basement, then the bottom floor and finally the top floor to no avail. They were amazed that the two women had killed all of the guards, the Senator and probably the Sheriff, Walt Long. One surprise was the stepmother's body. She had taken an overdose of sleeping pills.

They left the house, found the rest of their search team, and discovered they had come up empty also.

Bob told them, "You two take the houses on the east side of the community, and we'll take the west side. Be careful. We killed the worst of the scum, but who knows how much more there are that will want to take up where the Senator left off."

They had searched all but a couple of houses when Jack solemnly walked up to Bob and Will and said, "There's no good way to say this, but Jane was shot in the back and didn't survive...."

"No! Hell no!" Bob said as he fell to his knees.

"Maddie is okay and is with Jane. I'll take you to them."

Bob was still on his knees with Will crying as he tried to console his Papaw.

Suddenly Bob stood up and said, "We can't be crying and moping around Will. We have to set an example for the others. Let's go get our women and take them home."

Jack led them to the other side of the community to a yard barn in the backyard of the last house before the gate. Several of Jack's team were guarding the area. Bob and Will walked into the structure and saw Jane lying on the floor with Maddie asleep by her side. Will shook Maddie's arm, and she woke with a start and reached for her pistol.

"Maddie, it's me, Will. We're here to take you home."

"Will, hold me. Jane was shot while we were leaving dad's house. We killed the man who shot her. Take me home. I'm tired."

They carefully placed Jane in the back of the pickup with her head on Bob's lap. Will and Maddie sat in the cab with Maddie crying on Will's shoulder.

Will picked up his walkie-talkie and called for his dad, "Dad, this is Will. I've got more bad news. Grandma was shot last night and didn't make it. Bob is with her, and we're bringing her home now. Can you break the news to mom? I don't want her to see Grandma dead before she is told. Grandma died killing the Senator and his thugs."

"Oh shit. Is Maddie okay?"

"Yes. She is with me now, and we will be there in about half an hour."

"This will hit your Mom very hard after just losing Jake. I'll tell her and help her get through this."

"Dad, Lebanon is free of all of the tyrants. It was a large price to pay, but at least we can soon live in peace."

"Son, the loss will hit you sometime soon. You are pumped full of adrenaline and in a fight or flight mode. Be careful. I love you son."

"I love you too."

Will had time to reflect on the rest of the trip and made his mind up that from now on he would dedicate his life to eradicating the human vermin before they could harm Maddie or his family. Kill them all and let God sort them out was his new motto. He held Maddie, caressed her hair, and tried to convince himself that he could stop his mom and Maddie from taking up where his Grandma left off.

*

Chapter 12

Day 23 – 59 - Aftermath

Will took Maddie to their camper a few hours after they brought Jane's body back home. Maddie lay in Will's arms without talking for a long time before she said, "I've lost two moms in the last month and can't get my head wrapped around the losses. I think I might be in denial because I expect Mom and Jane to walk into the room at any minute."

"Baby, I know what you mean since I can't believe that Jake won't ever be at our table pestering Missy and me, and I miss Grandma so much. I'm afraid I'll break down any minute. I've made a vow to myself that keeps me going...."

Maddie interrupted and said, "I wonder if it's the same as mine. I vowed to become the Wraith and kill every son of a bitch that tries to hurt any of our family before they strike."

Will replied, "Let God sort them out."

They buried Jane next to Jake behind Bob's house under the big oak tree. Later that year Bob built a white picket fence around the graves.

Bob and Jo were still devastated, but Missy was still in shock since she was very close to her Grandma and had spent a great deal of time with her over the years. Losing her brother and Grandma was a one-two punch to the gut that rocked her back on her heels. She would take months to recover.

The family left the community funeral service for Jane and congregated on Bob's deck to remember their Grandmother, Mother, and Wife. Bob brought a tray out of the house with two bottles of Bourbon and a case of almost cold beer and said, "I'll be damned if we're going to cry and sulk; we need to celebrate Jake and Jane's life and remember them and always keep them in our hearts."

Jo filled her glass and said, "I remember when Mom first met Bill and said 'What the fuck do you see in him.' It took her several years to see the kind and gentle man that I fell in love with."

Will said, "I remember when Mom brought Jake home, and Missy was pissed because she wanted a baby sister. I was happy because it was now two boys against one girl."

Maddie said, "I remember the first words Momma Jane said when I met her. "Child, don't move. You've been hit in the head.""

They all laughed, and Will added, "At least you didn't hear her tell me to get my hand off your boobs."

Maddie laughed and replied, "I did. I was faking being asleep until I knew what kind of people y'all were. Will I immediately thought you were a perv."

Even Missy had laughed at her comment before she said, "I remember Grandma cussing when Jake drove her golf cart into the lake. She jumped in, saved Jake, and pulled the cart out with Grandpa's truck. Jake thought she was going to kill him. Instead, she took both of us out for ice cream and hid the keys to the cart."

Bob took a swallow of his whiskey and said, "About a year after Mary died and Jo invited me to Thanksgiving dinner she seated me next to her mother. I fell in love with her that night and felt guilty on the ride home the next day because I felt that I was cheating on Mary. It took way too long to get over that and join Jane as husband and wife. She was smart, beautiful, and very tough when she had to be."

Bob lifted his glass and said, "Jane, look up Mary in heaven and get to be friends. I'll try not to join you anytime soon, but even God needs someone to stir the shit up every now and then."

They all lifted their glasses, toasted Jane and Jake and never forgot them.

***

Jim Dickerson took over leadership of Lebanon until a fair election could be held, but the real reason for the delay was to root out any remaining friends of O'Berg. Lebanon was now down to less than four thousand people from a high of thirty-three thousand before the lights went out. Many had died from lack of medication, hunger, and the riots, but most just walked away hoping to find the FEMA camps.

The only good news from the Senator's occupation of Lebanon was that he forced most of the remaining people to put out gardens and gather all of the pigs, chickens, goats, and cows from the area west of Lebanon. With Lafayette, the Horseshoe, Pleasant Shade, and Jim's farmer's crops, the people in their group shouldn't starve once the crops came in. The problem was making it until then.

Bob resigned from his leadership position the day after Jane died to spend more time with his family and the community elected Jack to a one-year term as Mayor of the Horseshoe. Bob told Jack and his family that he would take assignments and lead combat teams as needed though he'd rather spend his time improving life in the Horseshoe.

Jo was asked to become the Police Chief but declined due to her grieving process. Harold Hunter took the Police Chief's job and made Ned his second in command.

Bob took over the construction of the remaining security walls, guard towers, and with Maddie and Will's help the general improvement of the infrastructure of the Horseshoe

There were now four communities grouped together for their long-term survival, the Horseshoe, Lebanon, Fayetteville, and Pleasant Shade. Even the now abandoned town of Dixon Springs had been annexed by the Horseshoe and every criminal, drug pusher and thug were run out of town or shot. The fly in the ointment was that the city of Hartsville controlled the bridge over the river between Lebanon and the other three.

About a month after freeing Lebanon, Ben proposed that they band together, force the crooked mayor out, and get the city to join their group.

Bob asked, "Do we have any actionable intelligence from Hartsville?

"Yes. I've had several of my men probing the town, and they report back that the mayor only has three dozen men on his side that keep the others in line. There were only 4,100 people living in the city before the shit hit the fan and now I guess there are less than 600," replied Ben.

Bob laughed and said, "A dozen thugs are keeping 600 people under control?"

Ben responded, "Yes. Three-fourths are women and children, and the rest see the mayor and Police Chief as their legitimate leaders. They don't have a clue that he has robbed them blind and killed over a quarter of their men for resisting his regime. He doles out the food and makes them work on the city's farms."

"Well, you are the military guy, how do we kick the mayor, and his henchmen out of the town without getting the people killed," asked Alice Jones from Pleasant Shade.

Ben replied, "I'd like to propose that we infiltrate the town with about twenty fighters and silently take out their leaders and police force."

Jim replied, "Sounds like a job for the Wraith."

Will choked as he watched a tear come to his Papaw's eye, and then said, "I think I know how to contact him."

Ben quickly turned and said, "How do you know how to communicate with him?"

"I think that the Wraith is in our community and that if we have a group meeting and just mention the problem the Wraith might act on his own."

Ben replied, "That might or might not happen, and we can't depend on this mythical crime fighter to solve our problems."

"Just trying to be helpful."

Ben went on to say, "I'll need several volunteers for sniper and infiltration duties. I'd like to have the team ready ten days from now."

They all agreed, and the meeting was adjourned.

Bob, Jack, and Will headed back to the Horseshoe from Lebanon and had to go through Hartsville. To avoid the ongoing conflict, they had begun giving the guards several cans of food each trip to allow them to go through the blockade and skirt around the city. They had to pay both trips so Bob handed the guards two cans of Spam, three cans of corn, and a large can of spinach. The guard waved them through, and they began the long trek around the city on the country roads. While this was occurring, Will chatted up the other guard and handed him something as they drove away.

As soon as the guards were out of sight, Will said, "There are four roadblocks that take up 16 guards out of the Mayor's tiny army. They could all be eliminated without any danger to the snipers. There are three men at the police station at all times and another two guarding the Mayor's house. My math says that with around the clock coverage that would be twenty-seven of the Mayor's army."

"How do you know this?"

"The Major isn't the only one who gathers information on the enemy. The other guard will tell you anything you want to know for a can of warm beer. I have been talking with him on every trip over here for the past month. The people are fed up with the Mayor and his bunch of crooks, but their guns were confiscated, and the Mayor shoots anyone who questions his authority. The guard and most of the citizens want us to kick the Mayor and his henchmen out."

"Why didn't you say anything in the meeting?"

"The General didn't want to hear from us kids."

Jack replied, "His mistake, but you could have told us the info."

"I just did."

Bob dropped Jack off and continued the conversation, "You're not thinking about attacking the Mayor's little army by yourself are you?"

"No. Papaw, I'm not going to attack them by myself."

"Okay, smart ass. You're not so big that I can't bend you over my knee and bust your ass. Who's in this with you?"

"Maddie, so far and I think Mom will join us."

"Why didn't you invite me?"

"I knew I wouldn't have to. Once you heard the plan, I knew you'd come to me."

"Asshole."

"That's Grandson Asshole."

"I want payback to all criminals, thugs, gang bangers, politicians, and crooks."

"Maddie and I vowed to wipe them off the Earth."

"Get your Mom to join us, and we will put four Wraiths onto the playing field."

It was an hour before supper, so Will went into the camper and found Maddie in the shower, trying to take a quick hot shower. Will had hung two of those solar shower bags above the trailer, and one could get a nice hot shower if they were quick about it. Maddie had just turned the shower on as Will entered and began shucking his clothes. Maddie saw him running at the small shower buck-naked and said, "Hurry up, the hot water won't last. They both barely fit in the tiny shower but immensely enjoyed bathing together. Will lathered her back, and then the rest of her body and then switched off with her as she reciprocated. The water was now only lukewarm, and they rinsed quickly to get the suds off before the bags ran out.

They stepped out of the shower just as the water ran low, quickly toweled each other off, and ran to their bed to make love before supper.

Later Maddie lay on top of Will as they kissed and talked about Will and Bob's trip.

"Papaw wants to join us on our rat killing mission. Maddie sat up on top of Will and said, "That's great. Now we just need your Mom, and we will have a force to be reckoned with."

Will pulled her down to his chest, kissed her, and said, "We need to forget killing thugs and practice making love again before supper. I love you and love being married to you."

Maddie kissed him and replied, "Perv. I knew you just wanted my body when you felt me up that first day while I was unconscious."

Will and Maddie were the last to join the family for supper and the last ones to the kitchen had to wash the dishes since they didn't help cook the meal or set the table.

"Darn, got to wash dishes again," Will said.

"You and Maddie could stop whatever you are doing and get here on time," said Missy as she grinned at Maddie.

"Maddie threw a roll at her and replied, "I like washing dishes."

Joan said, "Moving right along, how did the meeting in Lebanon go today?"

Bob replied, "It was a good meeting. We have four communities in our little group and Lebanon is cut off from the rest of us by that asshole Mayor in Hartsville."

Joan answered, "Well we need to cut out that damned pain in the ass. I'll volunteer."

"Lady, that's the plan. Too bad the Wraith has been on vacation, or it would have been taken care of by now."

Missy added, "Yes, he would have shot the Mayor and his men."

"Joan quickly said, "Who said the Wraith is a man. She could be a woman who wants justice and doesn't mind getting her hands dirty. Bob and Will trained me to shoot, fight with a knife, and kill with a compound bow. I'd love to get a crack at killing the men who...."

She looked over at Missy and finished the sentence, "Abused me."

Bob replied, "You've got a point there; there's nothing more dangerous than a momma bear protecting her cubs."

"Or a woman protecting her family. I sometimes wonder if y'all realize what a wonderful family that you have under this roof. You always have each other's backs. You work hard and play hard, and you always find a way to have fun even in trying times," Joan said.

She started crying when she realized that her family was probably dead and she was alone in the world. Bob and Jo both gave her a hug, and Jo said, "Joan you are a part of our family now, and can stay with us as long as you like."

Jo told Will to join the others on the deck while she and Maddie washed the dishes. He bolted for the door as Maddie threw a wet dishrag at him.

"Momma Jo, did you just break the single woman rule?"

"Nope. I have long range plans for Joan."

"Oh shit. You are going to hook her up with Bob."

"Shusssssh. I know Bob is heartbroken now, but in three to six months, the desire to find a mate will kick back in gear. As you know well things move at twice the speed of sound for relationships after the lights went out. A woman without a man is fair game for those creeps and outlaws. A man without a woman is a lonely miserable bastard who won't survive either. I just need to keep putting her attractive body in front of Bob every chance I get, and nature will take its course."

"You don't think she will make eyes at Bill or Will do you?"

"She wouldn't look at Will, but Bill is closer to her age. Our job is to stop that before it gets started. I don't think she will try for a married man with Bob and a few others around. Hell, she laughs at all of Bob's jokes and spends a lot of time with him alone. Hell, they might become friends with benefits if nothing else."

"You are evil. My kind of evil. You know Helen hasn't found a man either. Perhaps we sic both of them on Bob."

"Now that was pure evil. Maddie, I am so glad Will found you. He needs a strong woman, and I know you will make him happy."

"Mom, I love Will with all of my heart and soul. I want to be a great wife, but I'll never be subservient to anyone. We will be equal but bend to the other's needs when necessary. I love this family. Joan was right. This is a unique family, and I'm proud to be part of it."

"We're glad to have you in our family, and I couldn't have picked out a better mate for Will. Now back to match making. Let's figure out how to get Bob to take Joan down to the swimming hole by the rocks."

Maddie replied, "Skinny dipping?"

"No, we need to move slowly. Put them together whenever we can and make small suggestions that one might be interested in the other."

"Sounds like a plan."

*

Chapter 13

Day 60 – Return of the Wraiths

It was over a month, and a half since Jane, Jake, and Izzy were killed, and thankfully, things had calmed down a bit for the family. The crying had ceased, but the grieving process would go on for a while longer. The family was strong, so life had to go on since people had to eat, the land had to be farmed, and people had to move on.

Since Bob didn't want to move another camper onto his property, Joan stayed in one of his bedrooms. Maddie and Will still had one of the new modular homes and Bill, Jo, and Missy had another modular home. Joan cooked most of the meals, did the laundry, and house cleaning for Bob and the others as her contribution to the family. The entire family worked at jobs for the community and tended to their large garden after their day jobs.

It was late spring and warmer than usual for this time of the year in Middle Tennessee. The crops were growing well; they should have more than enough for themselves and be able to trade with the other communities for items they needed. The one setback continued to be the town of Hartsville.

Jo watched her son and his wife holding hands as they walked over to the house for breakfast and wondered what kind of life her grandkids would have in this post-apocalyptic world. She knew that with Walt and the Senator dead things would get better but also knew there were still plenty of criminals and thugs out there to plague them on down the road.

"Hey Maddie, bring Will over here for a minute."

"What's up Momma Jo?"

"No pressure, but how do you two feel about continuing Mom's work taking out the trash."

They both laughed, and Jo was surprised at the reaction and upset that they didn't take the subject seriously. Her face turned red, and she was about to walk away when Maddie replied, "I'm sorry, but the reason we laughed is that we were going to ask you to join us to finish Momma Jane's work. Will and I vowed to rid the Earth of all vermin, so our kids will have a safer and better life."

"You aren't....?"

"Not yet, but the pills have run out and the condoms won't last forever."

"Yeah, I'm not wild about giving Will another baby brother or sister. I talked with Doc about tying my tubes, and he is against it due to the risk of infection. Now he will do a vasectomy or neutering but nothing for us ladies."

Will grimaced and said, "I'll pass. Besides we want kids, just not now."

"Back to the subject; let's meet after breakfast to plan out our little adventure and make sure nothing goes south. Think about how to gather intelligence and long-range sniping. Let' go on to breakfast."

"Oh, by the way, Papaw is also joining us."

"That's great. Maddie, talk with Joan; I'll bet she will join our motley crew."

Will replied, "I think we can bring her up to speed quickly, but do we need five people?"

"Will, please this time just trust your Momma," replied Maddie, who then added, "She knows what she's doing."

"Son, I don't want to lose anyone. My plan is to have two people perform the close in work while the other three stand back under cover and protect the attacker's backs. Even if we are just sniping, I want several of us to watch for danger and prevent surprises."

Will said, "That makes sense. I'm in."

Maddie joined Joan to wash the dishes and started the conversation with, "Joan do you really think you could kill someone?"

"Maddie, thank God no one has ever raped or abused you. I want to kill every person who rapes, kills, or damages any person, and may there be a special place in hell for anyone who abuses children. Girl, I think killing is the last thing that should be done in a society of ordinary people; however, we are in a situation where society has broken down, and the people must eliminate the bad people and pray to God they know the difference."

"Then join our little team and start killing the bad guys. We're meeting at the swimming hole over by the rock bluff on the river. You can ride with Will and me. Bring something to swim in."

"I don't have anything."

"You're about my size. I have a couple of bikinis."

"Maddie, do you think that is appropriate?"

"It's either that or a t-shirt and shorts."

"I'll take the bikini. Who's on the team?"

"Jo, Will, Bob you and me. We are the Wraiths."

"Poor Bob is still grieving for Jane."

"We need to get his mind off Momma Jane and get on with life. He's a tough man with a big heart. He needs to grieve for another few weeks and get his ass back in the game. Men or women without a mate won't make it long in this world."

"Was there a message for me in that sentence?"

"Yep, dear teacher, you've been single for several years and need to pair up for safety, quality of life, and peace of mind."

"You are wise beyond your years. Could you introduce me to some of the single men in the community?"

"You live with the best one. Be patient and good things come to she who waits but works her magic."

"I was afraid the family would ask me to move out of Bob's house since we are now alone together."

"No, we think you are a keeper. I'll leave it at that."

They all went to work at their various jobs while Joan cleaned the house and tended to the garden. Bob arrived home from work first, and Joan had a cup of coffee and a beer waiting on him.

"Joan thanks for the coffee, but where did you get the beer. I only have a few cases of Bud Light left, and this is a full body ale."

"You are the first one to try my home brewed beer. Well, technically, it's ale, but the main point is that it is alcohol. I may be a lady, but I love my home brewed ale. My Dad always brewed his own at home, and I helped him growing up. Is it good?"

"Damn, Skippy. This is excellent. I'm not an alcoholic, but I also love my beer and whiskey."

"It's a bit green because I only let it ferment for three weeks."

"Can you make whiskey?"

"Yes, but I'll need someone with a good taste for whiskey to help me find the right aging and flavor. Moonshine is all I can start brewing. Bourbon gets its flavor from additives and the type of barrel it's aged in. Distillers actually burn the inside of the barrels to give whiskey flavor and color."

"Damn, we don't have any barrels."

"We can start with steel drums and add charred wood. It will take years to perfect the flavor, but what else do we have to do?"

Bob looked at Joan, smiled, and said, "I volunteer to be your helper and official taster."

"I accept your offer. We can start gathering the supplies and equipment over the next few weeks. When the crops come in, we will be able to improve the process. I can make vodka from potatoes and moonshine from corn, wheat, or about any grain. I also know how to make wine."

"Damn girl; if we make excess, we can trade it for other much-needed goods."

"Bob, that's part of the reason I started making the beer. We need medical supplies, hygiene products, and ammunition. The other reason is that I saw you were running out of beer and I want to contribute to the family however I can."

Joan surprised everyone with the ale for supper and was thanked by all.

Bill took a sip and exclaimed, "This is great. I hope there is more."

Joan replied, "There are another 39 bottles in this batch. I have to find bottles, mason jars, or even gallon jugs to put the ale into for consumption. Bob and I are teaming up to produce wine, beer, and whiskey. We all like to drink the stuff, but we can also trade it to other communities for things we need."

Jo kicked Maddie under the table, and Maddie smiled back at her. Matt was visiting Missy, so they were tasked with the dishes when most of the others made excuses and left. Bill had to go back to their small hospital to check on a kid with a fever. Will and Maddie were waiting on Joan to ride with them when Jo came out of the house walking with Joan who got in Bob's pickup and left with him.

"Mom, I guess you told Papaw about Joan."

"Yes, and they are riding together over to the swimming hole. Let's go."

Will thought for a minute and decided to keep his mouth shut because he knew that he didn't want to know what their devious plan was for his Papaw and Joan. Well, he did, but he didn't want to get involved.

Their cover story was that the family was out for a swim after a hard day's work. Bob brought a dozen cans of beer for the meeting, and all brought blankets and towels. As usual, Will and Bob walked down the rocky bluff to make sure the water was clear of logs or other dangers so they could jump off the cliff into the water. There were no dangers, so Will yelled to the women to jump in and join them. Maddie and Joan jumped into the cool water together followed by Jo. They swam for a while and then climbed back up to the top of the bluff so they could see anyone trying to approach.

Jo started the meeting by saying, "I guess we can all agree that our first operation should be clearing the trash from Hartsville."

Everyone agreed, and Bob added, "I think after we finish that one we should make a list of our priorities. I for one want to clear out a fifty-mile radius around the Horseshoe."

Joan added, "I agree, but I also want to find the boys who raped me and kill the sorry bastards."

"Joan, sorry, but who were the boys. Surely I know them," Maddie replied.

"It was that thug Ralph, Donnie, and Demarcus. Those boys always hung out together. I hope they are still together because I want to string them up by their balls and torture them before I kill them."

Jo was surprised by what Joan said and answered, "Was Donnie a skinny white kid and Demarcus a tall, heavy set black kid with a skull and bones tattoo on his neck?"

"Why yes, that's two of them. Do you know where they are?"

"In hell. They are the ones who hit Maddie on the head and stole our bikes. They headed south to Nashville and were killed by someone who wanted their bikes and supplies. I watched one of them die."

Joan began sobbing as Bob held her close to him trying to console her.

"I should be happy, but I wanted to kill the SOBs myself. I'll kill a dozen more of the scum to help someone else from being attacked," she said as she clung to Bob."

Bob replied, "Girl they're dead. Move on. There's plenty of criminals that need eradicating, besides a pretty girl like you needs to be chasing down some young man and having a family."

"I have a family, and they are all around me now."

"I meant a steady boyfriend who might make husband material," replied Bob.

"I have a man in mind. I just have to get his attention."

Bob laughed and said, "Just wear that bikini; if he's got blood, it will get him interested."

She laughed and said, "That's a good idea."

Jo whispered to Maddie, "She doesn't need our help. Bob will be following her around like a puppy dog in a couple of months."

Will sipped his beer, and then got the meeting back on track with, "We are having fun, but we need a plan. I think we take out all of the men at the roadblocks at the same time, then the police station, and then finally the Mayor and his bodyguards."

Jo disagreed, "I think we hit the Mayor and his henchmen first, and then kill the others from long range as they respond to the Mayor's house. I don't want the Mayor to slip out of town when the shit hits the fan."

Joan responded, "Why are we attacking them at all? I thought Ben and Jack's team were taking out Hartsville."

"Jo answered, "Because those two big men thought that women and children shouldn't be exposed to that kind of danger."

"Fuck him and the horse he rode in on," replied Bob.

"I see it's a challenge," Joan said.

"Yes. Mom started the Wraith, and we are going to keep the fear in all outlaws, perverts, and gang bangers. We will run them out of the area."

They spent another half hour discussing their plans and then headed back to the house for their customary nightcap on the back deck. Joan and Bob sat close together, as they drank their ale or sipped their whiskey and that made Jo happy for her father-in-law.

Jo caught Bob alone as everyone headed to their rooms for the night and said, "Pop, please don't grieve over my Mom too long. You are still too young to waste your life mourning. Death is around every corner so you should live life to its fullest."

"Jo, my mind agrees with you, but my heart is broken. I need just a little more time. I'm not blind or stupid. Joan was shaking her cute ass at me all afternoon in the skimpy bikini. She looks damn good, but I'm not ready."

"Don't take too long because other single men might like that bikini also."

"I'm not worried. She sat next to me, and I even flirted with her a bit. Joan and I are partners in a post-apocalyptic brewery and still. We will make damn good alcohol together for a while, and perhaps we'll.... Well, we'll do what we want to after that."

Two days later, they snuck out of their dwellings and met on the other side of Bob's barn, and then they walked a couple hundred yards to where they had staged Bob's pickup and another old pickup for the operation. Both had large cargo trailers behind them to help with their cover story. They drove to the gate, and Bob told the guards that they were heading over to Gallatin to check out some freight trains and warehouses for food and other supplies.

"Now Bob, you know Jack doesn't like anyone leaving after dark."

"You tell Jack that he ain't my daddy and this ain't no dictatorship. Now get the gate open, or we'll go through it."

"Don't get your panties in a wad. I'm opening the gate. Good luck and bring me something back."

"Will do, if we find anything."

It was a short drive over to Hartsville and the first roadblock. Bob made sure they arrived an hour before shift change at midnight. The plan was to divide into two groups with each group assigned to kill the guards at one of the roadblocks during shift change. That would take out eight of the guards, and then they would go kill the guards at the other two. That would take out 12 of the guards leaving four at home asleep and all of the roadblocks unmanned.

Maddie and Will were assigned to the roadblocks on the east and south side of the city, while Bob, Joan, and Jo had the ones on the north and west. Bob had Jane's suppressed .22 Ruger and Maddie had her AR15 with a suppressor.

Maddie and Will moved into position and Maddie watched the men for a few minutes, and then shot the first man in the heart. She then moved her scope to the other man and could only get a head shot. Her aim was true, and both guards were dead. They quickly ran over to the guards and staged them sitting down in their lawn chairs by the fire. Will placed his hat on the one with the bloody head and they both looked alive from a distance.

They only had to wait for a short while until the other guards appeared. They drove up in a small older car and got out to greet their comrades. Maddie shot the driver before his feet hit the ground and shot the other as he ran around the car to see why the driver had fallen. All four guards were dead, and the mission was successful so far.

Bob drove up to the guards at the north blockade and asked for directions. Only one guard walked over to the truck, so Bob offered them a shot of whiskey from his bottle. The one guard took a drink as the other one joined him for his share. Bob slid the Ruger above the window and shot both of them before they could react. Joan and Jo took their weapons and Bob finished them off with a headshot.

Joan gulped, ran to the bushes, and vomited everything in her stomach. Jo offered her a bottle of water and a handkerchief.

"Joan, every decent human being hates killing even when it has to be done. There is no shame in what you did."

"It's the first time I helped kill anyone."

"It won't be the last dear."

They sat the bodies' upright in their chairs and waited on the next crew. This time Joan asked if she could do the shooting.

"Are you are up to it?"

"Yes, Bob, I have to do it now if I will ever be of help to you."

"Okay, but if you freeze we'll have to slit their throats after a fight."

"I might puke my guts up afterward, but I won't freeze."

"Here's the Ruger; get as close as possible and shoot each one twice as quickly as possible," Bob said as he pulled his knife and added, "Jo and I will finish them off."

Joan unbuttoned her shirt and took it off to reveal her more than ample bosom covered only with a sports bra and said, "Those assholes will be looking at the girls and thinking about getting in my pants. I will shoot them and wipe their grins off their faces."

Joan sat down between the two dead guards and waited a few minutes before the guards walked up to the fire. Joan stood up, waved Bob's whiskey bottle, and said, "Your buddies and I partied a bit too much. They might need help getting home."

"Damn, where did you come from? You got any of that whiskey left?"

Joan walked over to the two men who were busy looking somewhat south of her eyes and raised the pistol. She rapidly shot both of them twice before they took their eyes off her breasts. Before Jo or Bob could get to her, she shot both men in the forehead.

"That's what they get for thinking with their dicks instead of their heads. I think I'm going to...."

She didn't move a step before she upchucked again until she had the dry heaves. Jo again, gave her water and a handkerchief to clean her mouth.

"Ya' done good girl," Bob said as he patted her on the back.

Bob then took a rag and dipped it in the pool of blood on the ground.

He then said, "Let's roll. Joan, Jo, we get the police station and should be right on schedule to eliminate those bastards at the same time Will and Maddie take out the Mayor."

The town was relatively small, so they walked down side streets and alleys to the police station and waited in the darkness until exactly 1:00 am before Bob dabbed some of the blood on Joan's right arm and laid a towel over her hand that was holding the .22 Ruger.

Bob and Jo helped Joan stagger into the front door to the station and Bob yelled for help. The two cops at the desk ran over to help, and a third came bursting through a door at the back of the room.

Bob yelled, "A bear mauled her over by the river."

All three cops were fixated on Joan when her pistol barked several times as Jo and Bob drew their pistols and finished the cops off.

"Please get this blood off me; that bastard could have had HIV or something."

Jo washed her arm off with soap and water while Bob found the first aid kit and a bottle of rubbing alcohol to finish cleaning her arm.

"Come on, let's move. We need to see if Will and Maddie need any help."

There were two sentries on guard outside the home and one inside. The one at the back door was asleep and Will cut his throat without a sound. The one at the front door was awake, but Maddie's suppressed rifle took him out without disturbing the neighborhood. They both snuck in the kitchen door and found the inside guard asleep on the couch. Will slit the man's throat while Maddie kept watch.

"Maddie, I don't want to chance killing anyone of the Mayor's family so I'll make a noise until the Mayor comes down to see what's happening and you can shoot the bastard."

"Works for me, but what happens if he doesn't come down. Bob said he was a real chicken shit."

"Then we go up and get him and try not to kill too many of his family."

Will knocked a chair over, which made a loud bang when it hit the kitchen floor. They heard some talking and then suddenly a man came running down the stairs with a baseball bat. Will stuck his rifle in front of the Mayor's feet and tripped him. He fell down the last six steps and landed on his head. Maddie kicked him, and he didn't move. He broke his neck during the fall and was dead.

They heard a noise and then a voice, "Are you okay you worthless prick. I hope you fell and broke your damn neck."

They choked down a laugh and left the house to go to the First Baptist Church to wait for the rest of the team. Bob, Joan, and Jo walked up ten minutes later and joined them inside the church.

"Well it's done, and none of us got hurt. Well, Joan almost got her boobs groped. It's time to call in the big dogs."

Bob pulled his long-range radio out of his pocket and called for Jim Dickerson, "Jim, do you copy?"

"This is Otto, his second in command. What do you need Bob?"

"Could y'all send over a couple of dozen troops to secure Hartsville? It appears that the Mayor and the police force all committed suicide last night. There are only a few of the bad guys left."

"That's good news. Did you help them with their suicides?"

"Oh no! Someone left messages from the Wraith telling the citizens to get rid of the rest of the scum."

"Okay, I'll pass it on and wake up the troops."

"Thanks."

"Can I write the message from the Wraith?"

"Joan, you are free to paint."

"Thanks, Bob."

There was a noise at the front of the church, and a man walked toward them in his robe.

"I'm the pastor of this church. Did I hear correctly that the Mayor and his thugs are all dead?"

"Yes, most are dead. A few cops are still in bed. We discovered the problem and asked for help in securing the town."

"But you didn't kill any of the criminals yourselves?"

"No, we're just passing through and saw the Wraith's message and tried to find someone in charge. We saw the dead people and stopped here to pray."

"I may be a pastor, but I know a load of bull when I smell it. That doesn't matter. All that matters is that my town is free again. Thank the Wraith for me."

Joan walked back into the church, and the pastor asked, "Is this the Wraith?"

"No, sir. I'm just a scared woman who serves God the best she can."

"Well, I won't tell anyone about seeing y'all today. May God go with you."

"Amen to that brother. Let's go."

*

Chapter 14

Day 75 – A Family Can Survive

Jo woke up before the others and looked at Bill lying in her arms. She wondered what would happen next to her family. Jo thought surely losing her son and mother would be enough, and God wouldn't ask this family to place another sacrifice on the altar of the apocalypse. Losing their home, jobs, and having to kill a dozen people to survive also took a toll on her family, but she knew they were growing stronger with each adversity.

Not everything had been horrible since the shit hit the fan. They had gained Maddie, who has been a great addition to the family and would make an excellent wife for her son. Missy's boyfriend Matt was a good find for Missy. He was her first serious boyfriend, and Jo just hoped they progressed a bit slower than Will and Maddie.

The people in the community, for the most part, were friends for life and enriched their day-to-day experience. Finally, there was Maddie's teacher Joan. It was too early to tell, but Jo hoped Bob and Joan would get together after he finished grieving over Jo's dead mother.

Jo couldn't go back to sleep, so she walked over to Bob's home and found Missy and Maddie sitting on the deck drinking coffee while watching the sun peek above the trees to the east. She poured her a cup just as Joan came out of her room stretching and yawning.

"Hey, please pour me a cup too," Joan said as she fetched a cup from the cabinet and joined Jo.

Good morning. I hope you slept better than I did last night."

"Actually I slept very well once Bob, and I finally went to our rooms for the evening. He is quite the storyteller, and I just wish I'd met him under different circumstances. He talked mostly about your mom last night and how much he missed her."

"Give him time and don't push him. Normally it would be a year or two before a man like Bob would be interested in a relationship, but these days things move along much faster."

"Oh, I won't push him at all. If I were out in the cold, I'd have to be in a hurry to find food and shelter. Working for my keep being Bob's maid isn't too bad."

They joined the girls on the deck and heard Maddie say, "I have a few ideas on how we can electrify our little community. We found several large generators with all of that construction equipment and one could easily supply 120 volt AC to Bob's house and our three trailers. Hell, with a couple of DC to AC converters we could power a dozen homes as long as they all didn't try to run air conditioners."

Bob walked into the conversation with his coffee cup and said, "Maddie, that's an excellent idea, and we can have it in operation in a couple of days. Now, who drank the last cup?"

Joan replied, "I'm sorry; I'll go make a fresh pot."

"Sit down. I already started a new pot and stuck the biscuits in the oven. That reminds me that we need to find more propane before we run out and have to cook on wood stoves."

Bill popped his head out the door and said, "Where's the food? Did I miss breakfast?"

Will was right behind his father and had a cup of coffee in his hand as he left the kitchen and walked out to the deck. He walked over to Maddie, kissed her, and sat down beside her, before saying a word.

"May I have your attention? It has come to me that we have been driven from our homes, attacked by criminals and politicians, and no one knows what normal is anymore. We need to take a break from fighting to survive and reflect on why we are trying to survive. We must also determine what our new normal is in this brave new world."

"Damn Will, you sound like a politician. Perhaps Maddie should bonk you on the head before you run for office."

"Yes, and I have a bonking hammer. Seriously we do need to begin having some type of normal day to day activities or the stress will kill us all."

Jo added, "We need to celebrate our old holidays and make them a day of rest. Memorial Day is next Monday. Let's have a community picnic, games, and a pig or goat roast."

They decided to have a Memorial Day celebration in the Horseshoe to remember the Veterans and friends that sacrificed their lives for the USA and the Horseshoe. The festival would be on the last Monday of the month, which was only six days away, and they would have BBQ, games, and a fishing derby. Mrs. Green took charge of the food preparation with Joan, Jo, and a couple of the other women assisting.

Missy and Matt took charge of the children's games and planned everything from checkers to a three-legged race.

Jack and Bob handled the fishing derby and decided there would be prizes for the largest fish and the most fish caught.

Maddie and Will were to lead a competition for the best ideas that would improve life in their community with Bob, Jack, and Harold being the judges. The ideas would be evaluated the morning of Memorial Day with prizes for first through third place awarded before dinner that evening.

Memorial Day morning started as usual with the Karr family gathered around Bob's deck and coffee pot. Everyone was in a good but reflective mood and needed the break from soldiering or farming. Bob cracked his usual jokes and picked on Missy that morning since it was her turn in the rotation. The breakfast was prepared by Joan with Missy and Maddie assisting and was lighter than usual since they were to pig out the rest of the day.

Missy, Will, and Maddie had guard duty until noon, so they quickly ate and drove out to their posts. Bill had to attend to a few patients that morning and left a few minutes after the rest with Jo tagging along. This left Joan and Bob sitting on the back porch enjoying their third cup of coffee.

"Bob I'm so jealous of you because you have this beautiful family that is made up of such down to earth great people."

Bob replied in a joking manner, "Yeah, I had to beat some sense into several of them when they were younger, but I think they have become good people. You know my son was a damn liberal before he came down here when the shit hit the fan."

"Bob, did you know that I was also a liberal before coming down here and still hold many of my liberal values."

"Darn, I thought you were too perfect. Smart, beautiful, and appreciates my corny jokes. Now even I have to say that all liberals aren't too bad, besides I have plenty of time to wear you down on some of that radical stuff."

"And I guess that means I have time to wear you down on some of that hard-headed conservative stuff. Perhaps we can meet in the middle one day."

"I need a little more time and patience from you, and we'll meet in the middle as often as possible. Just don't ever tell me you voted for Obama."

"I did, and I'm proud of it. I assume you voted for Trump."

"Yep, both terms. Hell yeah! Made America great again."

"So do you think there is hope for us in this crazy new world?"

"Yep, but we'd better avoid politics for a while. Oh, by the way, what religion are you?"

"I'm a backsliding Baptist as my father used to tell me."

"Well, we have something in common. I'm a Baptist who just got closer to the Lord when the bullets started flying. We can go to church together and let the church ladies talk about us living together."

"They already are."

The cooks delivered a delicious variety of meats, vegetables, and desserts for the get-together. Tony Fulkerson roasted a goat, Joan smoked several pork butts, and the other ladies delivered a mouth-watering assortment of fresh vegetables and deserts. There was an impromptu pie-baking contest won by Jack's daughter-in-law for an excellent chocolate meringue pie.

Missy and Matt entertained the kids with the three-legged race, water balloon toss, slip and slide, and shooting BB guns at targets for prizes. They all won awards and were plied with Kool-Aid and cookies.

The adults played horseshoes and corn hole for pies and cakes with the overall champion team being excused from guard duty for three days.

The winning idea for improving the community came from Jack's twelve-year-old grandson. His idea was to cut a channel across the top of the Horseshoe to allow the water to gush through the canal and turn a waterwheel that could turn a gristmill or turbine to make electricity. The elevation dropped over twenty feet from one side to the other of the Horseshoe on the north end.

The boy was awarded a Marlin lever action .22 rifle and a hundred bullets along with two dozen Oatmeal raisin cookies.

The judges and other community leaders were astounded that no one had thought of the idea before. Maddie challenged the leadership to conduct an ongoing program for the best ideas to improve lives and make the prizes larger to spur on the competition.

Second place went to Missy for her idea to make human powered electrical generators from old car generators and bicycles. Third place went to Ned's wife for a solar heating device to heat their homes utilizing old storm windows, empty cans, and black paint. There were numerous other ideas and about half would be used by the community. Maddie was charged with the responsibility to track the progress of each used idea and report to the leadership each week.

The day was a huge success, and everyone was dog tired but looking forward to the next celebration on the Fourth of July. Most of the people went home after they helped clean up the area, but the Karr family stayed until everything was cleaned and the games and cooking utensils were stored.

"Family, it's time to go home," Bob said and then Joan, and he got in his truck and headed to his house with the rest of the family in the back cracking jokes and telling stories.

They all went to their rooms, took showers and filtered back to Bob's deck for drinks and snacks stolen from the picnic. Bob and Joan were the first with drinks in their hands on the deck. They discussed how life was much calmer now and the family was all healthy and much less stressed. Bob told little stories about each of his family members living and deceased. He shed a couple of tears when he got to Jake and Jane.

Joan patted him on the back and said, "I'm glad I got to meet Jane and Jake while they were happy and interacting with everyone. Jane was a splendid person, and her shoes will be hard to fill. The Wraith is a legend for hundreds of miles I'll bet."

Bob looked at each one of his family and then asked everyone to pray with him, "Father in heaven, thank you for protecting those gathered here tonight. May they live long and prosperous lives while serving you and helping their fellow men. God, we've just sent some good people to join you in heaven, and I expect you to make them angels fighting evil in this world. Amen."

"Amen."

*

Chapter 15

Day 150 – FEMA – We're Here to Help You.

Jack asked Bob and Will to travel with him over to Lebanon and help represent the Horseshoe in a meeting with Ben and the rest of the community's leaders. Bob was reluctant at first, but Will talked him into the trip.

The sky was blue with only a few wisps of white clouds that morning. The rain stopped about midnight, and the air was so humid you could cut it with a knife. It was the first week of August, and it was already 84 degrees at 10:00 in the morning. Hot and humid in middle Tennessee was customary for the summer months, but this was too damned early to suit the people of the Horseshoe.

"I miss air-conditioning, but I wouldn't have found Maddie if the shit hadn't hit the fan," said Will as they bounced along in Bob's pickup on their way to Lebanon.

"I miss shopping and my iPhone," replied Maddie.

Bob thought for a minute and said, "I miss a lot of things we'll never see in my lifetime, but I love seeing my family grow stronger together and work toward the same common goals."

"Papaw, what do you think this mysterious meeting is all about," Will asked?

"I don't know, but it's been very calm and peaceful for the last four weeks and that shit ain't normal lately. My first guess is the shit is about to hit the fan somewhere close to us. My second is he is going to tell us we are dreaming and none of this happened."

Maddie thought for a few minutes and replied, "And Jake, Jane, and my mom would still be alive, but I wouldn't be married to my husband. Damn, nothing in life is simple."

Things had been going along very well in Middle Tennessee since Lebanon was freed from the Senator and Walt. It alarmed everyone when Ben called for an emergency of the four groups to be held in Lebanon at City Hall. He only told the leaders that there was an imminent danger and they needed to meet to decide how to handle the situation.

They arrived a bit early and visited with Jim Dickerson until the meeting was called in session.

Ben got right to the point as usual, "Men, I have just learned that there are several rogue FEMA and the Department of Homeland Security (DHS) groups in the southern part of the USA. These are filled with people who had worked in those groups and decided to seize power, take what they want, and form their own empires. The remnants of our military have been fighting them since the lights went out. One large group tried to force the Army to surrender Fort Gordon to them. That didn't go well for the DHS troops. They were massacred before they could mount an attack.

The problem is that the military is spread thin and is concentrated around the large cities or their bases. They have an enormous supply of weapons and ammo but hardly anyone to man the guns. Most soldiers went home to their families and never returned to their units. Therefore, I guess what I'm trying to lead you to is that a joint FEMA and DHS task force is heading our way to take over the Nashville area.

Bob asked, "So these groups want us to join them?"

Ben laughed and replied, "Yes, but they want us to lay down our weapons and become serfs working in the fields. They base their ruling model on old English Kingdoms where the king and noblemen have all the wealth, and the peasants work themselves to death and barely have enough food to feed their families."

"That shit won't fly down here. How big is the group heading our way?"

"They are a small splinter group from Atlanta that the main group is using to expand their territory. There will be 250-300 troops protecting another 100 or so civilians. They know about our community, and that's what gave them the idea to spread out much sooner than planned."

"So they think we will just roll over and let them make slaves of our families and us."

"Pretty much. They have Humvees with turret mounted machine guns, trucks, and a shit pot full of small arms they stole from the real DHS depot."

"How soon are they coming?"

"My source says they will have recon units in the area in a week or so posing as displaced people looking for food or jobs. The next wave of recon will test our security and resolve with small attacks made to look like criminals were trying to steal from us."

Jack asked, "Can we get help from any of the military branches?"

"Yes but not enough help. My friends in the Army are sending an infantry squad to help us prepare for the main attack. They arrive sometime next week. We're on our own until then. I need your help in developing a plan to repel and defeat the bastards," Ben answered.

"What will they do if none of their scouts report back and simply disappear," asked Will?

"They will keep sending out more scouts until they flood us with scouts."

"Then that will cause them to delay the main offensive, won't it," replied Will.

Ben said, "Yes, and it will give us the much needed time for the main Army force to arrive."

"Will, you hit the obvious button right on the damn head. Our plan is to get the communities watching for all strangers who look well fed and ask too many questions." Replied Ben.

Maddie asked, "Do we know their home base of operations for the central group or this splinter group?"

"Yes, we do. What's on your mind; that wasn't an idle question."

"Well, I've been listening to y'all soldier boys discussing how to defend our communities and all that came to mind was an offense is the best defense. Let's take the fight to their home base and families. Make them defend what they have taken until we can wipe them off the face of the Earth."

"Now young lady, let us professionals worry about the details and plans," replied Ben.

Bob and Will jumped up, and Bob said, "Wait a damn minute. I'd go into battle with this young woman over any of your soldiers. She has killed twice as many of our enemy than any three of your men. I think she is right about taking the fight to the rogue groups instead of sitting back and hoping the Army gets here before we are slaughtered."

"Maddie, I apologize for what I said. I'm old-school Army and not used to teenagers being in on planning significant operations. Now what I'm about to say is top secret and why I pushed back so hard on Maddie's suggestion.

The General in charge of our area has ordered a covert action that has several Special Forces teams starting a hit and run guerilla war with the rogue FEMA and DHS groups. They are recruiting locals to help keep the pressure on the groups by setting IEDs and long range sniping campaigns."

"That helps, but you must remember that we civilians make up over 95% of our little fighting force and belittling anyone of them could alienate the entire group," replied Will.

"Point taken and understood," so are y'all okay with the SF taking care of the main groups?"

Maddie replied, "Yes, that makes sense now that you explained the situation. I'm good."

They spent several more hours making assignments to the five communities. The Horseshoe was assigned the area from Dixon Springs down to the outskirts of Carthage along Highway 25. The Wraiths had cleared out all the gangs and drug dealers in the small community below the racetrack, making this new project much easier to set up.

"Bob, I know you've had some bad blows lately, but I need you to take on the rogue government spies heading our way so I can concentrate on building up our community's defenses."

"Jack, I'm good as I'll get for a year or so and I need something to help keep me from sulking in a corner. Killing a few scumbags will brighten my day."

"Great, just let me know how I can help or assist with supplies or people."

"The only thing I'll ask is that you let me do it my way. I'll need about ten good fighters from our community to join my force. I'll use Jo, Maddie, Will, and Joan plus what you give me. I'd like Tony, Harold, and Ned if you can get them to volunteer."

"I can't promise, but I'll twist some arms."

"Jack thanks for getting Harold, Tony, and Ted, but do you think Matt is up to this mission? I don't know the other five real well, but they all have military or police backgrounds. Hell, now Missy wants to go with us."

"Bob, you have told me many times that we have slid back in time to the old west days. Missy and Matt would be married and have a kid or two by now, and Matt would be expected to fight the Indians or other hostile forces. We need these teenagers to be ready to take over from us in the next ten to twenty years, and they won't be ready unless we train them and give them the experiences they need to survive."

"Damn, did you practice giving my speech? I know I've said all of that many times, but Jo has just lost Jake and Jane. I'm not sure if she can survive another loss."

"Why don't you ask her? Here she comes with Missy and Matt in tow."

"Pop, tell these two love birds that they will not be assigned to the same scout group."

Bob shook his head and said, "Jo, are you okay with Missy going on this mission?"

"Of course, how else is she going to learn; however, I don't want her and Matt playing grab ass when they need to be concentrating on watching for enemy activity."

"Mom!"

"Mrs. Karr!"

"Shut up! Start acting like adults or neither of you will go on this mission with us. Matt, you go with Harold. Missy, you go with your Mom. You obey their commands, or I'll horsewhip the both of you. Are you good with that?"

They both responded, "Yes, Sir!"

Bob waved for all of the team to join him at the picnic tables and told them what teams they were on for the mission.

"Joe has Missy and Zeb. They have Dixon Springs. Will has Maddie and Oren, and they have south of the Horseshoe across the river. Harrold has Matt and Sally, and they have the community south of the racetrack on Highway 25. Tony has Ted, Sue, and South Carthage. I have Joan and Shorty, and we'll take North Carthage. Our mission is to find the spies and capture or kill them. We would like to catch a few to interrogate, but I don't care if you kill most of them. They will try to blend into the locals but won't quite fit in as well as they want to.

Look around the tables. Harold, you have lost fifty pounds in two months, and you are lean and fit for the first time in twenty years. Hell, I've lost twenty pounds. The rest of you are gaunt, and even the women are well toned and a bit muscular. We don't overeat, and we work from dawn to dusk every day. I expect the spies have had it very easy for the past three months and will stand out if you look close enough. Any of the Walkers you will see are starving and filthy. Hell, they plumb stink. If you see a dirty person that doesn't stink it's probably one of the spies."

Harold added, "I think we should move out to the fringes of our area, blend in with the trusted locals, and watch for newcomers."

"That's exactly what I had in mind. You will only carry a hidden pistol and knife while keeping your rifle and other gear hidden in a safe place. Each group will have twenty sticks of dynamite, a .308 or .338 hunting rifle for sniping and food for a week. You'll keep your walkie-talkies hidden, and you will report to Jack at a set time for each group. If you miss two call-ins, we will send a team to rescue you. Set up a base in an abandoned barn or house close to your target area and don't tell the locals anything about your mission.

I wish we had a better way to find the bastards but using your common sense, noticing people who ask too many questions about our community, and keeping your eyes out for someone who doesn't quite fit in is all we have for now.," added Bob.

Joan walked away for a minute and came back with a small bag for each of the group.

She pulled a mason jar out of one of the bags and said, "Of course plying a stranger with some booze might help loosen their tongues. I have two mason jars full of moonshine from my first batch. Bob and I have cut it in half and mixed it with powdered orange juice and lemonade, and it tastes almost good and has a bite."

Bob added, "Save some for the intended purpose and don't drink it all on the first night. Now, any questions?"

There weren't any, so Bob said, "Jo, you head out with your team after lunch, and the rest of you leave here every two hours until all have left the Horseshoe. Happy hunting."

Will caught his Papaw and asked, "Oren is ten years older than I am; will he balk at taking orders from me?"

"Son, I talked to him and asked him that question, and he replied that he was a good soldier and would obey your orders. He did say that he would appreciate it if you would listen to his advice when he gives it."

"Of course I would listen to his advice, but Papaw you know the bottom line is I will do what I think is the right thing to do at the time."

"I'm counting on that, son."

Jo went back to her house and found Bill home alone since Missy and Matt went to his place until time to leave. She walked into the living room and heard the water running in the small bathroom; Bill was in the shower. She quickly stripped her clothes off and joined him in the lukewarm water.

"Hello, good looking. I knew if I waited long enough, a beautiful naked lady would join me in the shower."

"I'd better be the only naked woman in your shower," Jo replied and then led him to their bedroom.

An hour later, they lay on the bed wrapped up in each other's arms while they discussed the upcoming mission and their Gung Ho daughter.

Bill said, "I'm not comfortable with Missy going out on this raiding party even if she will be with you. Damn, she's only a teenager."

"She'll be 16 this month, and we have to get her ready to survive if something happens to us."

"I know all of that, but we just lost Jake, and she's my only little girl. I hate this screwed-up world that robs kids of their childhood."

"Bill, do you really think that Missy and Matt wouldn't be sneaking out behind our backs if they'd met before the lights went out?"

"Teens have sex all the time, and the smart ones don't get knocked up. I mean having to kill or be killed. I only wish my biggest fear was worrying if a boy had my baby girl in the back seat of a Mustang and not if she'd kill or be killed."

"Darling, make love to me again and get that out of your mind because there ain't a thing we can do but fight beside her and always have her back."

"The family that fights together stays together or something like that is our new motto. I'm sorry, but I'm not in the mood."

Jo quickly changed his mood and got him thinking about her instead of the screwed up world. She was ten minutes late leading her group off to war, but Bill had a big smile on his face the rest of the day.

While the spy hunting teams were getting their orders, Jack met with his team to further beef up the security at the Horseshoe and the newly annexed area to the east of the Horseshoe. This mainly consisted of adding more guard towers and some barbwire fences along with a cleared path across the top of the new area to give the tower guards an unobstructed field of fire.

Jack knew the goal was to expand their joint communities out to the surrounding area as time went on so permanent fortifications would be a waste of time. He wondered if they would ever get to a time where they wouldn't have to be on guard every minute of the day.

The first day of the mission was uneventful and most of the time was spent settling in at their base camps, hiding their gear, and making initial contacts with a few trusted local people.

Will's team drove the VW down Highway 25 after dark, hid the car in the woods and walked to an abandoned farmhouse about a half mile below where Pleasant Shade Road ends on Highway 25. They spent the first night setting up their observation post in the old house and hiding their gear. Oren took the first watch from 10:00 pm until midnight. Maddie had the second watch from midnight until 2:00. Will had the third watch from 2:00 until 4:00, when everyone would get ready to move out before daylight to their positions to observe the local people and determine what the regular routine was for the north end of Carthage.

Nothing unusual happened during Oren and Maddie's watches; however, about 3:45, Will saw someone heading across the woods with a flashlight in the dark to a barn. Then a few minutes later, he saw another flashlight bouncing along to the same barn from a different direction. Will woke Maddie and Oren up on schedule and asked Oren to stay behind while he and Maddie went to see what was going on in the barn. They walked carefully through the darkness and arrived at the barn in about 15 minutes.

Will and Maddie saw that one of the side doors was ajar on its hinges, so they went to the door and listened to tell what the people were doing.

"Shush, Will I hear movement and grunts. I think they are stealing some pigs," said Maddie.

"I don't know about that. I heard someone praying to God. Look there is a faint light, let's take a look."

They heard, "Oh God. Oh God," before seeing the naked couple doing what naked people do.

"Oh shit, they're screwing," Maddie said.

"Wait, we need to find out who they are. Pull back. I don't want to watch, but I want to hear their conversation. This isn't a husband and wife. This is two people cheating on their spouses, and that gives me an idea."

A short while later, Will said, "Come back and listen. You'll like this."

"You are a pervert."

"Come on and listen."

They heard the woman say, "Damn, that was good. If Henry catches us, we're dead."

"The man replied, "Hell if Ethyl catches me, she'll neuter me and kill you."

"Well, Mr. Assistant Police Chief you just need to keep fighting crime in this barn with me, and she'll never know."

"Are you still slipping Henry a sedative?"

"Yep, it works every time. He is happy because he gets more sleep lately."

Will nudged Maddie and said, "Let's move in."

"They don't have their clothes ...."

Will stood up, walked up beside the couple who were still naked and wrapped around each other and said," I just recorded your conversation, and you are going to help us, or I'll play you grunting and talking about cheating on your spouses to your spouses."

The man started for his service revolver when Maddie came up behind him and poked the business end of her AR15 to his head and said, "You can do what he says or die now. We just want your help and nothing more. I don't care if we shoot you or tell your wife. It's up to you. I'd rather have you listen to what we want you to do, and then decide if you want to live or die."

Will picked up his gun and searched their clothes before throwing the clothes on their laps.

The man replied, "I'll do anything to keep this secret."

"Okay, put your clothes on, and we'll talk."

They quickly dressed while Will and Maddie made sure they didn't try to escape or pull a fast one.

"Okay, we need you to be our spies in your community. We need to know if any strangers have drifted in and stayed. Stuff like that."

The man said, "That's all?"

Maddie said, "Yes. We don't care what you are doing, and you can keep screwing in this barn. We don't care; however, we expect you to tell us everything going on in North Carthage and as much as possible about what you hear from Carthage."

"Why do you want to know these things?"

Maddie replied, "We think some terrible people are going to filter into the area, learn about our communities, and then attack us and take what we have. You can help us find their spies and neutralize them before they attack."

"If we do this, you won't tell anyone about us?"

"We promise," Will said.

"Okay, we'll do what you want just, please don't pass this on. Hey, I just remembered that the Chief told me a couple of days ago that an officer from DHS showed up in town two days ago and he is showing the officer around the area this week."

Will answered, "Thanks, that's just the kind of info we need. The DHS guy might be the real deal, but there are also fake DHS people casing towns so they can take them over and make the people slaves to farm their plantations. Keep an eye on him and make up your own mind, but keep us informed on what you hear. We'll meet you both here at 5:00 every other morning so you can fill us in on anything new."

"We'll be here replied the woman.

"We'll it's nice to know that people still have their priorities in balance," Maddie joked with Will.

"Did you actually think I was going to watch them make love," Will asked?

"They were like two dogs in heat."

"I thought you didn't watch," replied Will.

Maddie pinched his side and replied," I'd rather do than watch anytime. That's one thing we'll need to catch up on when this mission is over."

"Damn, that hurt. Is sex all you think about," Will said as he got out of her reach? Now, seriously, we need to get back to Oren and report back about the DHS person."

Bob laughed and said, "You caught them doing what? Oh well, everybody needs a little loving every now and then."

Joan asked, "What was that about? What did Will catch someone doing?"

"The Assistant Police Chief was doing someone else's wife."

"I'll bet that was embarrassing for everyone."

"Especially the ones with the bare asses," Bob replied.

Bob, Joan, and Shorty drove the same route as Will had taken that day but went on further south and then east of the city by taking several back roads. Bob's goal was to get as close to the Smith County Police Station and Court House, which were in the same complex. The closest place they could find a place to base their operations was an abandoned mine just 300 yards north of the Jail.

Bob had received Will's report about the DHS person visiting Carthage, and the cheating cop and asked

Shorty, "Hey do you know anyone in the government in Carthage?"

"Hell, most of the people died months ago that I was friends with. I remember a man who worked with my wife a few years back who became a deputy sheriff. We played cards at his home one night, and I think I can find where he lived back then."

Bob answered, "Let's walk over to the Sheriff's Department and see if he is at work."

It was a short walk over to the Sheriff's office, and while they walked, Bob decided that they would just walk in as if they owned the place and ask to talk to the Sheriff. Bob would use the ruse that they were looking for a thief who had stolen a hog and headed south on Highway 25 toward Carthage.

"Hey, Bob, what's an old Army puke like you doing in a big city?"

Bob did a double take and saw the man who hailed him, "Well, if I ain't a monkey's uncle. It's my old friend George Pratt. What's a crooked supply Sarge doing in a one-horse town like Carthage?"

"The same story as most people have these days. I was managing a gun shop on Highway 41 Alternate just outside Fort Campbell when the shit hit the fan. We were attacked the third day, and the owner was killed, so I loaded up every gun and box of ammo I could get in my old deuce and a half and headed south. I'm working here part time as a deputy just for a place to live and three little meals a day. How about you and who is this beautiful lady," he replied as he kissed Joan's hand.

"Be careful George that lovely lady is my new girlfriend and I already claimed her," slipped out of Bob's mouth before he could stop. He went on to say, "Would you like to move down to our community? We need another Army puke to help with our security, and you would get your own place to live and great grub. There are also some more lovely single women there but none as pretty as mine," Bob said as he found Joan's hand in his.

"Are you sure? I don't want charity," George spoke as a smile came over his face.

Joan spoke up, "Bob's community took me in, and I can assure you that you will work your ass off, but everyone works, and everyone fights when needed."

"Damn, sign me up."

"I have George, and I just had a brainstorm. Could you take us to a place where we can talk?"

"Yes, I'm on a smoke break, and we can go out to the benches under the tree over there."

Bob filled George in on the Horseshoe, the recent events and their mission in Carthage while the others kept watch.

"You can leave for the Horseshoe now, but I'd like you to stay here and keep your ear to the ground for a while to see if the town is being infiltrated."

"I'll be glad to handle that for you. By the way, the Police Chief asked my boss if I could give this DHS asshole a tour of the area, which includes the Horseshoe. I met the man, and he seems more like a thug than a DHS government official. Too rough around the edges to suit me."

"That's great; the rest of us will snoop around the highways coming in and out of town for strangers. Hey Shorty, ask George if your friend is still in the area."

Shorty said, "Do you know Eddy Sikes?"

"Hell yes, I know that brown nosing SOB. Is he a close friend of yours?"

Shorty grimaced, as he replied, "No my wife used to work with him, and we played cards at his house once. I knew he was a deputy over here, so we were going to pump him for information."

George laughed and said, "If anyone has the scuttlebutt it would be Eddy. He has his nose six feet up the Mayor and Police Chief's asses. I don't like the bastard, but he will know what's going on if anyone does."

"Does he drink," asked Joan

"Like a fuc...err... fish. Pardon my French, young lady."

"George, I once was a lady; now I am one of Bob's warriors."

"And a pretty one I might say."

Joan replied, "Bob, George needs to meet Helen."

"I'm sure you can arrange that meeting," Bob answered, and then said, "George, she'll have you married in two months.

George laughed and said, "There are worse things that can happen to a man these days. I got to get back to work and my new spy job."

Bob handed him a walkie-talkie and said, "Call me every morning at 4:45 sharp until this mission is over."

Bob met with the Sheriff about the Hog, and afterward, the Sheriff took Bob over to the Mayor's office and introduced him to Edgar Lawrence the DHS officer assigned to this area.

"Hello, Mr. Karr, the Mayor, and Sheriff have told me a lot about you and what you have accomplished in such a short time. My mission is to scout the Middle Tennessee area and determine how FEMA and the DHS can help you survive until we get the country back on its feet. What does your community need the most?"

"Nothing from the government. The only thing you can do is to get the people north of us farming their own food instead of trying to steal our food. Every person in the USA needs to be growing their own food and ridding the country of all criminals. If you have seeds, guns, and ammo you could pass them out to the citizens, while the military roots out the criminals, gangs and want a be dictators trying to take other people's land and food."

"Well, we agree with most of what you say except for handing out guns. As I was telling the Sheriff, the President has declared martial law, and all but hunting guns are to be turned into the county officials so they can be picked up by the DHS."

Bob smiled and said, "Well lucky for me and my little community we only have a few squirrel guns and shotguns. You need to give us some M4s and Ma Deuces to fend off scumbags like Senator O'Berg and his henchmen."

"Sir, I'll have you know that the Senator is the reason that the Director of the DHS sent me out to Middle Tennessee. I am to meet with him and discuss his needs so he can govern and get this area back in the 21st century."

"Then you'll have to go to Hell."

"I beg your pardon."

"That's where the Senator is. Hell. He plundered and killed hundreds of the people around Lebanon, and they rose up and killed the worthless bastard. He was a crooked politician and thank God he was an incompetent crook as a dictator."

"Well, the Director will be very unhappy with my report."

Shorty took the first watch out on the road into the mine at 10:00. The air was a bit cooler when Bob felt someone lay down beside him and snuggle up to his back.

Bob said, "Damn, Shorty, you are supposed to be on guard duty."

Joan replied, "So you prefer Shorty to a naked woman in bed with you out under the stars?"

"Joan..."

"Bob..."

Shorty came back to camp a few hours later and saw them snuggled up together under a sheet on Bob's sleeping bag and let them sleep until wake up time at 4:00.

Bob woke to the sound of Shorty singing a country love song and found Joan's head on his chest as she struggled to wake up.

"I let you two love birds sleep through the night, and each of you owes me a turn at guard duty. Boss, it's 4:00 and I'm going to check the road again while you two put some clothes on your 'necked' bodies. There is some jerky, biscuits, and coffee for breakfast," Shorty laughed and said as he left the camp.

Bob rolled over, held Joan in his arms and said, "This was probably too soon for me to forget Jane, but I have grown fond of you and I really ain't good at the mushy stuff."

"Bob, you'll never forget Mary or Jane. I don't want you to push them out of your mind; I just want you to let me in."

"I think you got in last night."

"You know what I mean. In your heart, not just in your bed."

"Joan I care for you a lot. Just give me time, and I hear time cures all wounds. Do I need to give you a ring because we are going steady?"

"No, but I'm moving my things into your room when we get back."

"That will make tongues wag. I joke, but I don't care. I want you with me because you make me feel great and your smile brightens my day."

"George, when does the DHS officer want to see Lebanon or the Horseshoe?"

"That's funny that you ask, he's changed his plans and wants to see the Horseshoe and then Lebanon today and leave tomorrow without seeing the rest of the Middle Tennessee area. Something has him nervous as a cat in a room full of rocking chairs."

"We will head to the Horseshoe as soon as we finish talking. Try to get him to the Horseshoe no earlier than 9:00."

"Will do. See you shortly."

"Shorty do you feel comfortable visiting your old buddy Eddy today?"

"Yes, that shouldn't be a problem."

Bob handed Shorty one of the mason jars with the moonshine and said, "Perhaps this will loosen up his tongue a bit."

*

Chapter 16

Day 162 – Spy vs. Spy

Jack, Harold, and Jo met George and the DHS officer at the front gate and welcomed him to their community.

"I hear that you are from the government and you are here to help us," Jack said as he sneered at the man.

The officer looked around at the guards and the numerous weapons they carried and said, "It appears that you can protect yourselves, perhaps we can determine how we can discuss how we can work together to feed the massive amount of unfortunate souls that are starving in this area."

They drove out to the barn on Greg's property to meet, and Jack replied, "So we will trade them food for usable goods?"

"Well, no. They don't have anything of value because most are homeless."

"Oh, you mean the government is going to pay us for our crops?"

"Well no, but as US citizens you will gladly share your bounty with the less unfortunate."

Jack stopped the truck and led the Officer to the barn where Bob, Joan, and Jo joined them. The officer saw Bob and said, "I see you made it back home in time to meet with me."

Jack interrupted and said, "This fool thinks we will turn over most of our crops to the DHS to hand out to the starving masses."

Bob walked up to him and said, "Sit down and tell us all about how socialism and serfdom work."

The man slowly reached for a pistol hidden under his shirt when Bob quickly shoved the barrel of his .45 1911 into the man's forehead and said, "Move, and you will have two new holes in that dumbass head of yours. Jo, take his gun and frisk him."

Bob shoved the man down into a chair and bound his hands and feet to the chair before beginning the interrogation. The man turned white as a ghost, started to stutter when Bob slapped him across the face, and said, "Shut up unless I ask a question and then you'd better speak up and tell the truth. Now, who do you really work for?"

The man replied, "The DHS. I work for the DHS."

Bob punched him in the gut hard enough to make the man vomit down the front of his clothes, and then asked, "I'll ask again and don't lie, or the beatings will continue until you tell the truth. Who do you work for?"

The man winced and said, "Fuck you. I work for the DHS, and you are a dead man."

"Harold, I don't think this asshole understands that we mean business. Go get our little persuader."

"Okay Bob," Harold said as he left the room and quickly returned and said, "Ben hasn't been fed in a week. He's a bit weak, but he can eat, well, like a rat.

Harold showed the man the rat crawling around on the bottom of a five-gallon bucket and said, "We've notched the bucket on both sides so it will fit over your shoulders. We took bets on if he'll eat your ears or your eyes first. I've got a pint of moonshine that says the ears go first."

"You wouldn't do that. I'm a federal agent. The Army will wipe this place off the map."

Major Ben walked into the room in his uniform and said, "I'm the commander of the local garrison, and these men are volunteers with my force. I told them that my people would interrogate you, but they insisted they had much more efficient means to get the truth from you. I believe them now. Oh, by the way, I have a case of .556 bet on the rat eating your tongue first. Not to worry. You can always answer our questions with written answers."

"Fuck all of you."

"Harold, place the bucket over his head," yelled Bob.

The man went berserk as the bucket was flipped over his head onto his shoulders. The poor rat was scared to death and ran around his head as the man pissed his pants and begged for mercy.

"I'll talk. I'll talk."

"Remove the bucket."

Harold pulled the bucket off the man's head, and the rat ran down the front of his shirt biting him as he went. Harold reached down the man's shirt, caught the rodent by the tail, and left with the bucket and rat.

Bob sat down next to the man and said, "Tell me a story. Lie, and the rat comes back."

"Let me clean up first. I soiled myself."

"Yes and you smell like shit, but first we hear the truth."

"Okay, I was with the DHS until the Event. Then as everyone else did, I hid in the mountains of West Virginia until everything settled down. I ran into a friend of Senator O'Bergs, and he talked me into joining them in building their own country. They had a year's warning that this was going to happen but didn't know the exact date, and I think it caught them by surprise."

Bob asked, "How many troops and what type of weapons do you have?"

"There are 400-500 in the main force and several groups of 100-250 branching out to seize more area to farm. I am the point man for Middle Tennessee. They have pistols, M4s, and Humvees with machine guns."

Jack asked, "When will you report into your boss?"

"Not until I can get back to the West Virginia border, so make that four days. My radio won't reach that far, and I have to report in person so no one can intercept the report."

"When are they coming to our area?"

"There are half a dozen spies in the area now, but the larger group doesn't arrive until the end of the month."

Jack asked, "How can we find the spies?"

"There is a folded piece of paper in my wallet with the spies' names, locations and when I'm scheduled to meet with them tomorrow."

Bob smiled at Jack and said, "Bingo, then asked, "Do any of these spies know you or would recognize you?"

"No, I never met any of them."

Jo asked, "Will the fake DHS people bring their families?"

"Yes, but only after they have eliminated all threats and opposition. Each family will get 150 acres and ten men to work the land."

Bob gagged and said, "You mean they will make slaves out of us?"

"No, you will become indentured servants and get to keep a part of the crops you grow."

Bob was steaming as he asked, "How will you keep us from rebelling and overthrowing your sorry asses?"

"The men will have shackles on their legs, and the women and children will be held in work camps with armed guards. If you escape, they will kill your kids and later kill your wives."

Bob kicked the man backward, drew his .45, and shot the man between the eyes as he fell back.

Harold yelled, "Damn I didn't see that coming."

Jo choked and said, "I did, and it still sickens me to see a man's brains blown out the back of his head."

Joan walked outside, leaned up against the barn, and puked until nothing came up anymore. Jo went over to her with a bottle of water and said, "I'm sorry you had to see that. Bob is usually very kind and sweet."

"Jo, I love Bob just the way he is and wouldn't change him. He has the guts to do the hard tasks. I'm not as strong as the rest of you, but I'll do what it takes to make sure no one harms our family. I might puke afterward, but I'll do my job."

"You are strong because you can do what's needed. Hell, I've been a cop for many years and still vomit when I see someone killed. I also think my Mom would be pleased that Bob has met someone who will love him and work with him to protect our family."

"Thanks, that means so much to me."

Bob came over, took Joan in his arms, and walked her to his truck so he could take her home. As he left, he said, "Let's meet at my home after lunch so we can send teams to go interrogate and eliminate the spies."

Shorty's man, Eddy, was a treasure trove of information about the questions asked by the fake DHS agent and had one fact that surprised everyone.

Shorty reported, "Bob, Eddy says one of his fellow deputies was on a routine patrol and ran across a camp in the woods with about twenty men dressed in black battle dress uniforms. They were armed with M4s, side arms, and turret mounted SAWs on top of three up-armored Humvees. They also have one five-ton truck with a trailer."

"Mr. DHS failed to tell us that little tidbit."

"My friend went on to say that he reported it to the Sheriff and was told that he must not tell anyone about the men because of national security."

"Thanks, Shorty. Now, we know the Sheriff, and probably the Mayor know about the DHS, but what we don't know is if they know these are fake DHS or have been fooled."

Ben had a worried look on his face and said, "We have to take out the men in the camp and the six spies now. Those Saws could wipe us out in a frontal assault so we need a plan to kill as many as possible before they can react."

Bob thought for a minute and said, "Jack's team should eliminate the spies, and Ben your men plus some of us should take out the troops. We have four or five proficient snipers that could decimate their ranks quickly while your guys do their thing."

Jack replied, "I agree. We could probably find a way to kill them all but would lose too many people doing the job. I'll kill the spies and leave the heavy lifting to Ben and his crew."

"I'll take you up on the snipers and any other experienced fighters to help mop them up when we hit the main group. I don't want any of them escaping."

"Papaw, this is Will."

"Go Will."

"You were right. I chased down the Assistant Police Chief, and he filled me in on what he knows and what he suspects. First, the Mayor and Sheriff are working with the DHS man and have been promised high positions in the new territory he is to be in charge of after all resistance has been eliminated. Second, they may not know if he is fake, but they are in bed with him on killing any people who resist and placing the general population into work camps. Papaw, these assholes have to go."

"Will, take them out tonight and then get your team back to the Horseshoe. We have a problem to attend to in the near future, and I need your help."

"I won't fail you."

"I know son."

Bob called all of the other teams back to the Horseshoe to give them their assignments. They met that afternoon without Will's team, and Jack made the following assignments for the spy hit teams:

Jack's Team   – Will and Sally

Harold's Team – Zeb and Shorty

Bob's Team   – Tony and Joan

Snipers assigned to Ben – Jo, Maddie, Oren, and Ted

Others assigned to Ben – Matt, Sue, and Helen

Jim Dickerson brought 39 men and women from his team to join Ben along with the five men from Pleasant Shade. Ben brought four of his soldiers and 15 men and women from Lafayette for a total of 66 fighters plus 4 Snipers for a total of 70 against about 20 of the fake DHS.

Will waited until he saw the Mayor's lights go out in his office and had the team follow him and his guard out the back door to his truck. It was about 10:00 and they were able to stay in the shadows as they approached the Mayor. Will had the bodyguard in his sights when Maddie and Oren launched themselves at the Mayor. Will shot the man twice in the chest and then once in the head as the man lay on the ground. Oren cut the Mayor's jugular, and then they hid the bodies under a pile of garbage behind a nearby store.

Maddie hung a sign around the Mayor's neck that said, **"This criminal has been executed by the Wraith."**

They walked a few blocks over to the Police Chief's house, and Will threw a nice chunk of venison laced with sleeping pills over the fence to the Doberman. They waited for half an hour, and Oren picked the back door lock to allow them entrance to the kitchen.

The Police Chief lived by himself, so they were shocked when they heard a lady's voice coming from the bedroom. They listened, "Fred, I was doing my duty this morning when we were interrupted by two people who want us to spy on the DHS and local officials."

"What the ...? They caught you screwing Allan?"

"Yes, he is going to do the spying for them and screw up your plans to take over Middle Tennessee with that ex-DHS thug. Aren't you glad you had me spying on him?"

"Why the hell did you wait until now to tell me now? I have that asshole thinking that I believe he is from the DHS and I don't mind his guys doing the killing so I can keep my hands clean. We need to...."

Maddie walked into the room and shot both twice in the chest and once in the head with Jane's silenced .22. Will took the duct tape from his backpack along with the quart jar of gasoline and fashioned a time-delayed bomb by suspending the jar several feet above the hardwood floor with the duct tape and linking another piece about a foot long into the tape holding the jar in the air.

The duct tape burned slow enough to allow them to be a block away when the burning tape burned up to the tape holding the jar. The tape burned through, fell to the floor spilling its contents on the floor, and the liquid spread to cover a large portion of the floor. The vapor from the gas rose a few feet to the flame and ignited with a large explosive force blowing the windows out in a shower of glass. The house erupted in flames and was totally engulfed in a few minutes. The bodies were burned beyond recognition, but the whole town knew who the mysterious woman's body was by the end of the week.

"Let's go home and get some sleep before the next mission, "Will said as they climbed into the old VW.

"Another dead thug another dollar," replied Oren.

"I'm tired and want to sleep in my own bed tonight," added Maddie, who then said, "I'll bet we have some sleepless nights coming up pretty soon."

Bob and Joan waited up for Will's team to get back home after dropping Oren off at his house.

"Son, how did it go?"

"Both are dead, and we heard the Mayor and his mistress both admit that they knew there was a scam going on with the fake DHS. The Mayor planned to double cross the DHS officer and become the leader of the new territory."

"Well, get some sleep. Tomorrow is a big day. Maddie, Missy, and your Mom are joining Ben's team on the assault on the fake DHS troops while you join Jack taking out two of the spies. Harold and I will lead teams to kill the other four. Good night."

***

The next morning the hit teams went out to find the spies. Harold walked right up to the first spy with a piece of paper in his hand and said, "I'm here; give me your report."

The man looked a bit confused until Shorty stuck his pistol in the man's back and said, "Reach for the sky."

The man tried to draw his gun, but Zeb had his AR already aimed at the man and shot him in the shoulder from 50 feet. The man spun backward and hit the ground bleeding out before they could question him. Harold searched his body while Shorty and Zeb searched the cabin he was hiding in during his stay in Hartsville.

They found several maps of the area and a list of people to watch. Bob and Jim Dickerson's names were at the top of the list.

Harold took his team on over to Lebanon and encountered much the same scenario when he confronted the man. The only difference was that Harold raised his pistol first, but the man still tried to kill Harold, and again Zeb shot the man. This time Zeb got fancy and hit the man on the upper arm, and they were able to place a tourniquet on him and saved his life.

The spy refused to talk until Shorty placed the pointy end of his hunting knife into the man's arm and wiggled it around for a few seconds.

"I don't know anything; I was sent here to get information on the people on the list in my shirt pocket. Three of us were working with a DHS Agent named Al who was based in Lebanon, and the other three were working with another DSH agent located in Carthage."

"How soon will they attack this area?"

"Attack? We are coming here to help you."

Harold asked a few more questions, got what he wanted and cut the man's throat. Harold reported to Ben and Bob about the extra DHS agent, and Jim Dickson sent a team over to find, question and kill the bastard.

Jack's team found their targets, questioned them, and quickly dispatched them before heading home that evening.

Bob's team was the only one that met any real resistance. The first spy was happy to give up and spill the beans until the knife headed to his throat. He was quite pissed off that he did what was asked of him and still got the knife. The second man knew instantly something was wrong because he had worked with his contact several times before.

He drew as soon as Bob walked up, began shooting his 9mm at Bob, and jumped behind a tractor. He hit Bob on the left calf, saw Joan sneaking up on him, and shot her in the right hip knocking her down. Tony charged the man with his AR blazing away and got the guy with a lucky shot to the head. Tony wasn't hit by any bullets but slipped and fell into the tractor during his heroic charge. He saved Joan's life by distracting the spy from finishing her off.

Joan applied pressure to her wound and crawled over to check on Tony and Bob. Bob had a flesh wound and applied pressure to both holes in his calf before crawling over to Joan.

"Babe, are you okay?"

"I got a groove on my hip, but I think I'll live. The bleeding has stopped. What about you," she said as she lifted Tony's head onto her lap.

"I took one in my calf. The bleeding has stopped, but I'll need Bill and the Doc to patch me up. What about Tony?"

"He saved my life, killed this asshole, and then slipped and fell into the tractor. He hit his head on the way down and knocked himself out. He's got a big bump, but I don't see any severe damage."

"Bullshit, my head is pounding. There must be a significant dent in it."

Bob replied, "There is a major dent in the tractor. That farmer will want you to get it fixed. We need to get the hell out of here before he catches us."

"Screw you, Bob. I hurt too much to laugh."

***

Ben met with Jim and Jo an hour before the attack on the DHS troops was to begin. He had a map of the area northeast of Carthage laid out on the hood of a pickup and said, "My troops will come up from the west side of Highway 263 while Jim's hide along the north side of Highway 85 just north of the 263 junctions. They should cut and run toward you, and you will begin firing at will as soon as you see them. Jim, remember to let them get even with you, so you'll be shooting toward the east, so you don't kill my men coming from the south.

Jo, I want your snipers placed on the south side of this ridge so you will have a good view of their Humvees. Kill anyone who tries to man those machine guns. We can take them on and defeat them, but we'll lose a lot fewer men if you deny them access to the machine guns.

Now the tricky part. I must have three to five survivors to interrogate. Can you help me do that? I don't care if they are wounded as long as they can talk. Hell if they all throw down their weapons we'll take them alive so we can gain some intel on the main group."

Jo replied, "We'll do our job. They won't get to the Humvees.

Jim said, "We'll hold the line and ambush the bastards when you drive them our way."

"Maddie set up over there beside Oren. Ted, you and Sally, set up on the left end of the ridge and Sue come with me to the right end. Remember we hold our fire until we hear the Major fire the first shot. When you hear the shot, shoot any enemy target but concentrate on men trying to man the Humvees. Got it? Okay, now line up your first target and be ready to squeeze the trigger when you hear the shot."

They were approximately a hundred yards from the Humvees and Jo was surprised the group didn't have any perimeter guards out in the woods. They had several guards along the road on both ends of their camp. Jo's team was anxious to get on with the battle and get it over with as soon as possible. The suspense was nerve racking.

There was a shot coming from their left, everyone pulled their trigger simultaneously, and four men and two women dropped to the ground. Several men ran to Humvees, but they were cut to the ground by Jo's snipers.

Gunfire erupted east of their position, and the few remaining DHS troops ran north for their lives. Jo kept her people guarding the Humvees. No one in the group was injured. Jo used her scope to count the bodies and saw they had killed or wounded fourteen men and two women. Jo, Ted, and Sally walked down to the wounded, took their arms, and secured them to trees while they treated their wounds. The man had been hit in the shoulder above his body armor. The woman had been shot twice in the chest, but her body armor stopped the bullets even if she had been knocked on her ass.

Jo kept the other three on guard as they gathered all of the weapons, body armor that wasn't shot full of holes, and all documents from the bodies. She had all of the items placed in her new Humvee. She figured the Horseshoe should get at least one of the vehicles. She also moved half the ammo from the other two vehicles to her Humvee.

A few minutes later one of the Major's men waved as he approached and yelled, "Don't shoot. The Major wants you to know that we have been successful. All but five are dead, and we are questioning them now. You can go back to your homes, and we'll take it from here."

Jo replied, "That's great news, and we'll leave now for home. Tell the Major we kept one of the Humvees. Oh, what do we do with these two?"

The soldier turned and shot each one in the head and then said, "Not a problem. We were giving one to you and Jim's group and keeping the other one."

The soldier turned and left to rejoin his unit when Maddie said, "He killed them in cold blood, and who the heck is the Major to tell us that we can keep one of the three Humvees that we captured?"

Jo replied, "Play nice. Team, we don't have a prison or spare food for these criminals. Let's take our new toys home and check on our families."

＊

Chapter 17

Day 162 – Crispy Critters

Bob and Jack were delighted they now possessed a Humvee with twin .556 SAWs. They had seen Ben's team use them effectively several times to stop hordes of walkers and a biker gang. They quickly met and passed on the details of each operation and went to their homes.

The family spent the day before licking their wounds, digging out bullets, and applying bandages. Bob had been wounded before, so it was no big deal except they were light on painkillers, so he only took some aspirin to dull the pain. Joan's wound on her hip wasn't severe but hurt like hell. Bill gave her two hydrocodone tablets and rubbed some antibiotic cream on the wound.

Bob and Joan excused themselves and went to Bob's room for the rest of the day.

The family was sitting on the deck sipping some sweet tea after supper when Bob and Joan hobbled out to the deck followed by Missy who said, "Joan do we call you Mamaw or Grandma?"

Bob said, "What?"

"I saw you two coming out of your bedroom and just assumed we have a new Grandma."

"Damn, you are getting to be a bigger smartass than your brother."

"Joan jumped in and said, "First, Bob and I are together. Second, no one could replace your Grandma. Fourth, I love Bob. Fifth, call me Joan."

Bob looked over at Matt, who had his arms wrapped around Missy and said, "Damn, boy, you are around here pawing on my Grand Daughter all the time. Has Jo given you her sex talk?"

"Papaw, Matt doesn't need a sex talk."

"This is the one that says if you have sex with her daughter she's going to shoot his ass," Bob laughed and took a drink.

Bill replied, "Pop, Matt, and I had that talk a while back. He promised to be a good boy until they get married next month."

They were all drinking beer or whiskey except Joan to celebrate Missy's engagement because the hydrocodones made her a bit sleepy, so she stuck to the tea while Bob sweetened his tea with some moonshine. They were swapping war stories when there were several loud explosions that shook the earth and rattled windows and dishes. Bob pointed to the east and said, "Those sounded like nuclear bombs have been detonated about twenty miles from here. Who in the world would blow up farmland between Carthage and Cookeville?"

Joan pointed at the skyline and said, "Look, a large black cloud is rising in the east."

"Damn, that's not any mushroom cloud from an A-Bomb. Look at that sucker roll as it goes up to the sky. Shit, there are two different ones that are joining together."

"What could have caused that," asked Joan.

"Normally, I'd say a large gasoline or oil tank exploded. Son of a bitch. I'll bet it was an air-fuel bomb."

Bob got on the radio and called for Ben who responded, "I'll bet you are calling about our little explosion east of here."

"Damn Skippy. What the fuck was that and was anyone hurt?"

"Those explosions were three homemade air fuel bombs dropped from Army transport aircraft. We caught the enemy by surprise and wiped them out in a single minute. There are over 500 of the assholes who became crispy critters before they could fire a shot."

"Do what? I thought we had several weeks before they would get here and the Army would beat them here by a week."

"I'm sorry for misleading you, but there never was any large Army force freed up to help us in the fight. Until a week ago, I was secretly making plans for all of us to bug out to another location. I finally found a Colonel in Georgia, who had planes, fuel, and some brilliant near do well engineers and demolition folks who made the bombs. I couldn't tell you because we couldn't let the plans leak out. I trust you but we also trusted Greg, and you see what happened there."

"You used us as bait!"

"Well... "

"Son of a bitch. You had us stir the assholes up and head this way just to make sure they would attempt to roll right over us without proper tactical procedures."

"Yes, that about sums it up, but remember we wiped them out, and they can't hurt your family, and you get to stay at the Horseshoe."

"You tortured those men in front of the ones who escaped to send a message back to the main force. Shit, you even let them run, didn't you?

"Well, yes. We had to make sure they felt over confident and would roll toward you thinking it would be a piece of cake. They left themselves open to a mass slaughter, and it worked. Our plan was so good that the General used the same tactics on the main group and several of the splinter groups. We wiped out over 5,000 of the enemy in the last twenty-four hours."

"You would have sacrificed my family to succeed."

"No, we knew we could kill 90 percent of them, or I would have told you to get the hell out of dodge. Look I understand that you want to whip my ass right now but think this through and then look me in the eye and tell me you would have done differently. We fried all of the fake DHS and the threat is over."

"You mean until the next dictator comes along."

"No, we are rebuilding our armed forces, and with some help from our communities we will station troops with each community and build a force large enough to destroy these dictators before they can get a foothold."

Bob laid the walkie-talkie down and said, "I guess you heard what I said, so I'll fill you in on what the Major told me."

The family was both pissed at the Army and excited to be free of the looming menace at the same time as they continued to watch the black cloud grow for an hour and then slowly dissipate over the next several hours. The cloud had disappeared as the sun went down, and Bob had calmed down a bit. He hadn't threatened to kick the Major's ass for about an hour and was drinking a bit more beer than usual as they reflected on their lives since the shit hit the fan.

Bob walked back out onto the deck later that night and said, "We have some big decisions to make in the next week or so because I don't know if we can defend the Horseshoe against those big organized groups. By being successful, we have placed a target on our backs for one dictator or another to try and take what's ours."

Bill replied, "Can't we move on west or south and start over once the crops are in, and we could take plenty of food and seeds with us to start over?"

"Pop, won't there be other dictators, gangs, and assholes trying to take our stuff anywhere we go?"

"Jo, I think you nailed it. Eighty percent of the people in the civilized world have died off by now, and the O'Bergs of the world think they can be the king of a small country. I don't think leaving is the answer. I have changed my mind and believe we should grow larger, get better military hardware, and align ourselves with the new US Military forces that Ben's team is a part of."

"So we will keep fighting forever," asked Joan?

"No hon, not forever, but for a while longer," Bob replied, and then added, "We have to train every member of our community in the skills necessary to fight and survive so that we are so strong that nobody wants to mess with us. Let the Wraiths run free to eliminate the criminals and have an army large enough to be feared by the evil and needed by the good people. We should farm every inch of the land to be generous with our friends and trade with our neighbors. We will help anyone who wants to live in peace to get vehicles, power plants, and solar heating working in their communities. We will be a force for good."

"Papaw that was quite a speech you just gave; now where do we sign up for this brave new world. Maddie and I are expecting a son in about six or seven months, and I want him, or her, to grow up and not worry about survival or fighting all of the time. Let's get the trash taken out before the next generation grows up and has to deal with the mess."

The End

Thanks for reading my novel and please don't forget to give it a great review on Amazon.

AJ Newman

Read <u>Book 1 of my War Dogs</u> series – Heading Home.

War Dogs Heading Home - Book 1 of 3

Post-Apocalyptic Sci-Fi survival Fiction

Severely wounded Staff Sergeant Jason Walker and his Military Working Dog, MMax, are being shipped home. An EMP blast causes their plane to crash. Having survived two disasters, they face the Apocalypse and the struggle to get home. Will there be anything left to return to?

Ebook, Paperback, and audio.- Narrated by Roger Wayne

Read <u>Prepper's Apocalypse – Book 1 of 3</u> of my Prepper's Apocalypse series.

Prepper's Apocalypse Book 1 of 3

Tom's and his family's vacation ended with a devastating EMP attack on the USA during his family's return flight from Hawaii to San Francisco. Surviving the plane crash only caused them to confront the chaos of the apocalypse head-on. Their fellow survivors were helpless and lacked the skills to survive. Tom, his sister, and their grandma endure the perilous trip from San Francisco to their ranch in Southern Oregon, using their prepper skills to keep them alive during the anarchy and chaos around them.

Read <u>Book 1 of my Old Man's Apocalypse</u> series – Old Man's War – Book 1 of Old Man's Apocalypse

The apocalypse slowly rolled across the world without much notice. There weren't any bombs, EMP blasts, grid failure, or natural disasters to blame, as you always find in those post-apocalyptic novels. Jeff Mann had read dozens of those apocalyptic sci-fi novels, and all were wrong. The cause was the incompetence of the world's governments and the failure of the many Ponzi scheme cryptocurrencies. First, the riots came, and then starvation and depravity followed. The billionaires built safe compounds while everyone else died off or fought to survive the holocaust at the end of the modern world. After saving two young women from slavers, Jeff begins a crusade against human trafficking. Can one man and two women make a difference in a world gone mad?

Thanks for reading my novels.

Please leave a great review on Amazon. Thanks

Remember to read my other books on Amazon.

AJ Newman

To contact or follow the author, please like my page and leave comments at https://www.facebook.com/aj.newmanauthor.5?ref=bookmarks

For you MeWe folks: https://mewe.com/i/anthonynewman5

To view other books by AJ Newman, go to Amazon to my author's page:

http://www.amazon.com/-/e/B00HT84V6U

A list of my other books follows at the end.

Thanks, AJ Newman

*

Books by AJ Newman

Old Man's Apocalypse:
Old Man's War
Old Man's Journey

Prepper's Apocalypse
Prepper's Apocalypse
Prepper's Apocalypse: Collapse
Prepper's Apocalypse: Betrayal

John Logan Mysteries" The Human Syndrome

Extinction Level Event
Extinction
Immune: The Hunted

War Dogs
Heading Home
No One Left Behind
Amazon Warriors

EMP:
Perfect Storm
Chaos in the Storm

Cole's Saga series:
Cole's Saga
FEMA WARS

American Apocalypse:
American Survivor
Descent into Darkness
Reign of Darkness
Rising from the Apocalypse

After the Solar Flare:
Alone in the Apocalypse

Adventures in the Apocalypse

Alien Apocalypse:
The Virus
Surviving

A Family's Apocalypse Series:
Cities on Fire
Family Survival

The Day America Died:
New Beginnings
Old Enemies
Frozen Apocalypse

The Adventures of Jon Harris:
Surviving
Hell in the Homeland
Tyranny in the Homeland
Revenge in the Homeland
Apocalypse in the Homeland
John Returns

AJ Newman and Mack Norman
Rogue's Apocalypse:
Rogues Origin
Rogues Rising
Rogues Journey

A Samantha Jones Murder Mystery:
Where the Girls Are Buried
Who Killed the Girls?

These books are available on Amazon:
https://www.amazon.com/AJ-Newman/e/B00HT84V6U/ref=dp_byline_cont_ebooks_1

To contact the Author, please leave comments @
https://www.facebook.com/aj.newmanauthor.5?ref=bookmarks

About the Author

AJ Newman is the author of 39 science fiction and mystery novels plus 14 audiobooks that have been published on Amazon and Audible. He was born and raised in a small town in the western part of Kentucky. His Dad taught him how to handle guns very early in life, and he and his best friend Mike spent summers shooting .22 rifles and fishing.

Reading is his passion, and he read every book he could get his hands on. He fell in love with science fiction. He graduated from USI with a degree in Chemistry. He made a career working in manufacturing and logistics, but he always fancied himself as an author.

AJ served six years in the Army National Guard in an armored unit and spent six years performing every function on M48 and M60 army tanks. This gave him great respect for our veterans who lay their lives on the line to protect our country and freedoms.

AJ resides in Henderson, Kentucky, with his wife Patsy and their four tiny Shih Tzu's, Sammy, Cotton, Callie, and Benny. All except Benny are rescue dogs.

Made in the USA
Las Vegas, NV
24 January 2022

42203463R00152